American Stories & Poems for Children

American Stories & Poems for Children

SELECTED BY

Celia Barker Lottridge

National Library of Canada Cataloguing in Publication Data available upon request

ISBN: 1-55263-385-3

THE CANADA COUNCIL | LE CONSEIL DES ARTS
FOR THE ARTS | DU CANADA
SINCE 1957 | DEPUIS 1957

ONTARIO ARTS COUNCIL
CONSEIL DES ARTS DE L'ONTARIO

 The publisher gratefully acknowledges the support of the Canada Council for the Arts and the Ontario Arts Council for its publishing program.
We acknowledge the financial support of the Government of Canada through the Book Publishing Industry Development Program (BPIDP) for our publishing activities.

Key Porter Books Limited
70 The Esplanade
Toronto, Ontario
Canada M5E 1R2

www.keyporter.com

Cover design: Peter Maher

Printed and bound in Hong Kong

01 02 03 04 05 06 6 5 4 3 2 1

CONTENTS

INTRODUCTION   8

Once Upon a Time

THE LITTLE SCARRED ONE
Caroline Cunningham   12
RIP VAN WINKLE
Washington Irving   18
NANCY HANKS 1784–1818
Rosemary Carr and Stephen Vincent Benét   33
PECOS BILL
Traditional   34
CAP GARLAND
Laura Ingalls Wilder   42
JACK AND THE NORTH WEST WIND
Richard Chase   58
BEING NEIGHBORLY
Louisa May Alcott   70
PIRATES
Mark Twain   86
HIAWATHA'S CHILDHOOD
H.W. Longfellow   96
ASHES OF ROSES
Kate Douglas Wiggin   100
THE WIND BEGUN TO ROCK THE GRASS
Emily Dickinson   117

All Kinds of People

THE CONTESTS AT COWLICK
Richard Kennedy   120
THE PETERKINS ARE OBLIGED TO MOVE
Lucretia P. Hale   128
LITTLE ORPHANT ANNIE
James Whitcomb Riley   138
HARASSING MISS HARRIS
Katherine Paterson   140
WAY DOWN IN THE MUSIC
Eloise Greenfield   147
AFTERNOON ON A HILL
Edna St. Vincent Millay   148
A PUPPY FOR HARVEY
Betsy Byars   150
MY PEOPLE
Langston Hughes   157

All Kinds of Animals

COYOTE AND WATER SERPENT
Traditional   160
CUNNING BRER RABBIT
Traditional   168
THE WONDERFUL OX
Wallace Wadsworth   172
THE RUNAWAY
Robert Frost   178

HENRY AND RIBS
Beverly Cleary   180
THE ISLAND
Walter Farley   194
ZEBRA QUESTION
Shel Silverstein   205

Fantastic Worlds

THE HUCKABUCK FAMILY AND HOW THEY RAISED
POPCORN IN NEBRASKA AND QUIT AND CAME BACK
Carl Sandburg   208
THE TALE OF CUSTARD THE DRAGON
Ogden Nash   214
THE SCARECROW AND THE TIN WOODMAN
L. Frank Baum   218
AN IRRITATING CREATURE
Jack Prelutsky   226
THE POT CHILD
Jane Yolen   228
LONESOME BOY
Arna Bontemps   236
SLIPPERS
Laurence Yep   250

About the Authors   258
The Illustrators   265
Acknowledgments   266
Index   270

People living in the United States of America have always created stories and poems that have entertained and delighted children. Over the years, and particularly in the last 150 years, a vast literature has grown. In fact, the stories, novels and poetry that comprise American writing for children can, and do, fill large libraries.

In this volume, you will find a selection of the best-loved and most memorable stories and poems from this rich tradition. Although some of the selections were not originally written for children, girls and boys have adopted them as their own. Others are excerpts from novels, but they can be read as stories, too.

I like to think of American literature for children as a rambling house with endless corridors and hallways lined with doors. Behind each door lies the world created by a story or a poem. This anthology will lead you to some of the most interesting doors of all. Open any one and discover an old friend or step into a new adventure.

Through the oldest doors, you will find yourself in the American past — in a native American village, a one-room schoolhouse in New England, or a new town on the open prairies. You will find that while some ways of life have changed, other things about families, friends and school have hardly changed at all.

Behind many of the doors, you will meet memorable people. There's Wally, who outsmarts one of the worst bad guys in the West, and the Peterkins, an eccentric Massachusetts family who just can't seem to do anything right. A young boy discovers friendship in an unexpected place, while an angry girl finds that she has something in common with a person she thinks she hates.

You will also find remarkable animals waiting for you, from a giant blue ox to a talkative zebra. The black stallion that saves Alec's life is certainly a horse, but not like any horse you have ever known. Ribs, on the other hand, is like a hundred other dogs, but he is special in his own way, too.

Some of the worlds you will discover behind these doors may seem unbelievable. What about a popcorn farm where all the corn pops and threatens to cover everything, even the house? Or a house in the woods that disappears, along with a ballroom full of people, when the sun rises?

On the doors you will find the names of the creators of all these places, people and creatures. Some have been well known for a long time — Louisa May Alcott, Mark Twain, Laura Ingalls Wilder and L. Frank Baum. Others are contemporary writers, still adding to the richness of American writing for children. They are all worth knowing.

Letters to the Wind will open many doors on many worlds. Happy exploring.

ONCE UPON A TIME

CAROLINE CUNNINGHAM

THE LITTLE SCARRED ONE

IN days long go, a young Indian brave lived with his sister on the border of a lovely lake in the north country. She took care of his lodge, which was the finest one in the whole region. He was tall and handsome and all the Indian girls wished to marry him. He was guarded by a good spirit who had given him a magic arrow, so he caught more game than anyone else.

The spirit also had made it possible for him to be invisible when he wished, to everyone but his sister and the girl who would some day come with the power to see him. This girl he would know was the one intended to be his wife.

Toward evening when the sun was low, the Invisible One always returned home from hunting. His canoe came across the water as lightly as a leaf in the breeze. Then his sister would walk down to the shore of the lake with any girl who might have come to the lodge that day in the hope of seeing him.

To his sister he was always visible, and as his canoe approached the shore she would ask: "Do you see my brother?" Sometimes the girls would truthfully answer: "No." Oftener the word would be: "Yes." Then the sister would say: "What is his shoulder-strap made of?"

There were only two things the Indians used in making shoulder-straps: either a strip of raw-hide or a green withe from an ash tree. Sometimes a girl would answer, "It's made of raw-hide"; or sometimes, "The withe of an ash tree."

Knowing that her companion who said either of these things had not told the truth, the sister would reply quietly and kindly: "Come, let us return to the wigwam."

Some of the girls would stay to help cook the supper. They would wait with great curiosity to see the hunter eat. There was proof enough that he was a real person, for his moccasins, as he took them off, at once became visible and his sister would put them away.

Beyond this, however, the girls could see nothing, though many of them remained all night. Try as hard as they could, no one but his sister had ever seen the young brave.

Now, in a village at the extreme end of the lake there lived an old Indian with his three daughters. The mother was dead, so there was no one to see that the youngest girl got her share of everything. The child's bright eyes were sad with care. Often tears ran down her cheeks as she went for water or gathered wood.

She was a timid little thing, though very beautiful. Her sisters were jealous and hated her. They made her stay in a dark corner at the back of the lodge where no one could ever look at her. But she passed her time arranging beads and sewing them on her sisters' clothes in patterns like the flowers of earth and the stars of heaven.

When their father was away on his hunting trips the two elder sisters were very cruel; they abused her in every way they could think of, and made her sweep up all the hot ashes. She was small and weak and often ill, but this did not prevent them from treating her with great unkindness. Finally her body was scarred and her hair was singed, and the people in the village called her the Little Scarred One.

When her father would return and see her burns, he would ask: "How did this happen, my little one?" But she was afraid of her sisters and dared not tell him.

"Oh, it is all her own fault," the eldest sister would say. "We tell her not to go near the fire, but she always disobeys us and plays in the hot ashes. We can't keep her away."

The Little Scarred One was very lonely. She would sit by the lake at night, longing for her mother to come back to her. "I want my mother, I'm so lonesome," she would sob to herself. But her mother never came back.

One day it entered the heads of the two elder sisters to try their luck at seeing the Invisible One. They dressed themselves in their finest clothes, for they wished to look their best.

On reaching the lodge, they found the young brave's sister at home, and at sunset they went with her along the accustomed walk to the water's edge. When her brother approached in his canoe, she asked them if they saw him, and both answered: "Certainly."

They lied like many others. One said the shoulder-strap was made of raw-hide, and the other said it was an ash withe.

So they, too, had to return to the lodge without seeing him. But they stayed on and on, hoping to catch a glimpse of him while he was eating.

They saw his game drop to the ground at the door. They saw his moccasins after he had taken them off. But when he ate, the food became invisible as soon as he touched it. So the two girls had to go home angry and disappointed.

They were more cruel than ever to the Little Scarred One.

The next morning their father returned, bringing with him a great many pretty shells. The older sisters were soon busy stringing them, and the little girl begged for a few. The eldest refused, but the other one threw her a handful.

The Little Scarred One knew where her sisters had been, and she thought dreamily: "Maybe — maybe *I* could see him. Then how many things might happen!"

But she had no pretty clothes. She was almost in rags. What could she do?

The poor child had always gone barefoot. So she had to take a pair of her father's moccasins and put them in water to make them smaller and softer and easier to wear.

Near by, a silver birch stood, dressed in its beautiful white bark, and she thought: "Maybe my mother's spirit has entered the birch tree," for the Indians believed that every created thing had an indwelling spirit. She asked for just enough of the birch tree's covering to make a dress

and leggings. She drew some figures on it by scraping and peeling the bark, and then made the dress. In this odd apparel, wearing her father's moccasins and with a few strings of shells wound about her head because she had no beautiful braids, the strange little creature went forth bravely to try her luck.

For even the Little Scarred One wished to see the wondrous hunter in the great wigwam at the other end of the lake.

Her sisters called after her jeeringly: "Come back, come back, you silly little thing!"

As she passed through the village, the children and even the men and women laughed and hooted. Some of them said sadly: "Go back, Little Scarred One. It's no use." But she went on. For she had made a great resolve. Maybe it was the spirit in the birch tree that had inspired her.

When the poor little girl in her clothing of bark, with hair singed and her face scarred, reached the hunter's lodge, his sister received her most kindly, for she knew more than the mere outside of things as the world knows them.

At sunset the two girls went down to the shore. Off in the distance sounded the faint drip-drip, drip-drip of the brother's canoe-paddle. He was coming! They stood shading their eyes from the flush of the sun as they gazed across the lake. At last the sister said, "Do you see him now?"

The Little Scarred One replied with awe, "Yes, truly I do see him. He is wonderful."

"Then tell me what his shoulder-strap is made of," the sister asked searchingly.

"It is the Rainbow," she said. And great fear came upon her.

"But what is his bow-string?" asked the young hunter's sister.

"His bow-string is the Milky Way — the bridge of souls," answered the Little Scarred One.

"Truly you have seen him," said his sister. "Now we must go back to the lodge and prepare for his coming."

The two girls hurried home. The sister opened a chest of treasures in which lay the most beautiful clothes the Little Scarred One had ever seen, though at the thought of herself she hung her head in sorrow.

But the sister bathed her in magic water and a wonderful thing happened as the water touched her: all the scars vanished from her face and body. The sister combed her hair and under the comb it grew long and shining, like a blackbird's wing. Her eyes shone like stars. In all the world there was no such beauty.

The sister dressed the Little Scarred One in a wedding garment and adorned her with precious shells. She placed her in the wife's seat next to the door and the two waited.

At last they heard the game drop to the ground outside the lodge. The skins hanging at the doorway were drawn aside and there stood the Invisible One, handsome and wonderful. He smiled down upon the Little Scarred One kindly and said:

"So we have found each other!"

"Yes," she answered, shyly and worshipfully.

In the blue cool of evening, as the sun was setting beneath the edge of the world and the red was turning to black, the Little Scarred One became the wife of the hunter. They were married under a silver birch tree just by speaking a word — as is the Indian custom. The butterflies knew her and fluttered about. Flowers blossomed in the fragrant night air and greeted her with their scent-laden murmurs as she passed back into the wigwam.

RIP VAN WINKLE

Rip Van Winkle lives in the Catskill Mountains before the Revolutionary War in a village founded by the Dutch. He is a good-natured fellow and a great favorite of the village children, but he is a trial to his wife because he has no interest in work. To get away from her constant complaining, Rip often takes his dog, Wolf, into the mountains for a day of hunting and peace.

I N a long ramble of the kind of a fine autumnal day, Rip had unconsciously scrambled to one of the highest parts of the Kaatskill Mountains. He was after his favorite sport of squirrel shooting, and the still solitudes had echoed and re-echoed with the reports of his gun. Panting and fatigued, he threw himself, late in the afternoon, on a green knoll, covered with mountain herbage, that crowned the brow of a precipice. From an opening between the trees he could overlook all the lower country for many a mile of rich woodland. He saw at a distance the lordly Hudson, far, far below him, moving on its silent but majestic course, with the reflection of a purple cloud or the sail of a lagging bark here and there sleeping on its glassy bosom, and at last losing itself in the blue highlands.

On the other side he looked down into a deep mountain glen, wild, lonely, and shagged, the bottom filled with fragments from the impending cliffs, and scarcely lighted by the reflected rays of the setting sun. For some time Rip lay musing on this scene. Evening was gradually advancing; the mountains began to throw their long blue shadows over the valleys. He saw that it would be dark long before he could reach the village, and he heaved a heavy sigh when he thought of encountering the terrors of Dame Van Winkle.

As he was about to descend, he heard a voice from a distance, hallooing, "Rip Van Winkle! Rip Van Winkle!" He looked around, but could

see nothing but a crow winging its solitary flight across the mountain. He thought his fancy must have deceived him, and turned again to descend, when he heard the same cry ring through the still evening air, "Rip Van Winkle! Rip Van Winkle!" At the same time Wolf bristled up his back and, giving a low growl, skulked to his master's side, looking fearfully down into the glen. Rip now felt a vague apprehension stealing over him; he looked anxiously in the same direction and perceived a strange figure slowly toiling up the rocks, and bending under the weight of something he carried on his back. He was surprised to see any human being in this lonely and unfrequented place, but supposing it to be some one of the neighborhood in need of his assistance, he hastened down to yield it.

On nearer approach he was still more surprised at the singularity of the stranger's appearance. He was a short, square-built old fellow, with thick, bushy hair and a grizzled beard. His dress was of the antique Dutch fashion — a cloth jerkin strapped around the waist and several pairs of breeches, the outer one of ample volume, decorated with rows of buttons down the sides and bunches at the knees. He bore on his shoulder a stout keg that seemed full of liquor, and made signs for Rip to approach and assist him with the load. Though rather shy and distrustful of this new acquaintance, Rip complied with his usual alacrity, and mutually relieving one another, they clambered up a narrow gully, apparently the dry bed of a mountain torrent. As they ascended, Rip every now and then heard long rolling peals, like distant thunder, that seemed to issue out of a deep ravine, or rather cleft, between lofty rocks, toward which their rugged path conducted. He paused for an instant, but supposing it to be the muttering of one of those transient thunder showers which often take place in mountain heights, he proceeded. Passing through the ravine, they came to a hollow, like a small amphitheater, surrounded by perpendicular precipices, over the brinks of which impending trees shot their branches, so that you only caught glimpses of the azure sky and the bright evening cloud. During the whole time, Rip and his companion had labored on in silence, for though the former marveled greatly what could be the object of carrying a keg of liquor up this wild mountain, yet there was something strange and incomprehensible about the unknown that inspired awe and checked familiarity.

On entering the amphitheater new objects of wonder were to be seen. On a level spot in the center was a company of odd-looking personages playing at ninepins. They were dressed in a quaint, outlandish fashion; some wore short doublets, others jerkins, with long knives in their belts, and most of them had enormous breeches, of similar style with that of the guide's. Their visages, too, were peculiar; one had a large beard, broad face, and small piggish eyes, the face of another seemed to consist entirely of nose and was surmounted by a white sugarloaf hat set off with a little red cock's tail. They all had beards, of various shapes and colors. There was one who seemed to be the commander. He was a stout old gentleman, with a weather-beaten countenance; he wore a laced doublet, broad belt and hanger, high-crowned hat and feather, red stockings, and high-heeled shoes, with roses in them. The whole group reminded Rip of the figures in an old Flemish painting, in the parlor of Dominie Van Shaick, the village parson, and which had been brought over from Holland at the time of the settlement.

What seemed particularly odd to Rip was that though these folks were evidently amusing themselves, yet they maintained the gravest faces, the most mysterious silence, and were, withal, the most melancholy party of pleasure he had ever witnessed. Nothing interrupted the stillness of the scene but the noise of the balls, which, whenever they were rolled, echoed along the mountains like rumbling peals of thunder.

As Rip and his companion approached them, they suddenly desisted from their play and stared at him with such fixed, statuelike gaze and such strange, uncouth, lackluster countenances that his heart turned within him and his knees smote together. His companion now emptied the contents of the keg into large flagons and made signs to him to wait upon the company. He obeyed with fear and trembling; they quaffed the liquor in profound silence and then returned to their game.

By degrees Rip's awe and apprehension subsided. He even ventured, when no eye was fixed upon him, to taste the beverage, which he found had much of the flavor of excellent Hollands. He was naturally a thirsty soul and was soon tempted to repeat the draft. One taste provoked another; and he reiterated his visits to the flagon so often that at length his senses were overpowered, his eyes swam in his head, his head gradually declined, and he fell into a deep sleep.

On waking, he found himself on the green knoll whence he had first seen the old man of the glen. He rubbed his eyes — it was a bright, sunny morning. The birds were hopping and twittering among the bushes, and the eagle was wheeling aloft and breasting the pure mountain breeze. "Surely," thought Rip, "I have not slept here all night." He recalled the occurrences before he fell asleep. The strange man with a keg of liquor — the mountain ravine — the wild retreat among the rocks — the woebegone party at ninepins — the flagon — "Oh! That flagon! That wicked flagon!" thought Rip. "What excuse shall I make to Dame Van Winkle?"

He looked around for his gun, but in place of the clean, well-oiled fowling piece he found an old firelock lying by him, the barrel encrusted with rust, the lock falling off, and the stock worm-eaten. He now suspected that the grave roysters of the mountain had put a trick upon him, and, having dosed him with liquor, had robbed him of his gun. Wolf, too, had disappeared, but he might have strayed away after a squirrel or partridge. He whistled after him and shouted his name, but all in vain; the echoes repeated his whistle and shout, but no dog was to be seen.

He determined to revisit the scene of the last evening's gambol, and if he met with any of the party, to demand his dog and gun. As he rose to walk, he found himself stiff in the joints and wanting in his usual activity. "These mountain beds do not agree with me," thought Rip, "and if this frolic should lay me up with a fit of the rheumatism, I shall have a blessed time with Dame Van Winkle." With some difficulty he got down into the glen; he found the gully up which he and his companion had ascended the preceding evening, but to his astonishment a mountain stream was now foaming down it, leaping from rock to rock and filling the glen with babbling murmurs. He, however, made shift to scramble up its sides, working his toilsome way through thickets of birch, sassafras, and witch hazel, and sometimes tripped up or entangled by the wild grapevines that twisted their coils or tendrils from tree to tree and spread a kind of network in his path.

At length he reached to where the ravine had opened through the cliffs to the amphitheater but no traces of such opening remained. The rocks presented a high, impenetrable wall over which the torrent came tumbling in a sheet of feathery foam and fell into a broad, deep basin, black from the shadows of the surrounding forest. Here, then, poor Rip was brought to a stand. He again called and whistled after his dog; he was only answered by the cawing of a flock of idle crows, sporting high in air about a dry tree that overhung a sunny precipice, and who, secure

in their elevation, seemed to look down and scoff at the poor man's perplexities. What was to be done? The morning was passing away, and Rip felt famished for want of his breakfast. He grieved to give up his dog and gun; he dreaded to meet his wife, but it would not do to starve among the mountains. He shook his head, shouldered the rusty firelock, and, with a heart full of trouble and anxiety, turned his steps homeward.

As he approached the village he met a number of people, but none whom he knew, which somewhat surprised him, for he had thought himself acquainted with every one in the country around. Their dress, too, was of a different fashion from that to which he was accustomed. They all stared at him with equal marks of surprise, and whenever they cast their eyes upon him invariably stroked their chins. The constant recurrence of this gesture induced Rip, involuntarily, to do the same, when, to his astonishment, he found his beard had grown a foot long!

He had now entered the skirts of the village. A troop of strange children ran at his heels, hooting after him and pointing at his gray beard. The dogs, too, not one of which he recognized for an old acquaintance, barked at him as he passed. The very village was altered; it was larger and more populous. There were rows of houses which he had never seen before, and those which had been his familiar haunts had disappeared. Strange names were over the doors — strange faces at the windows — everything was strange. His mind now misgave him; he began to doubt whether both he and the world around him were not bewitched. Surely this was his native village, which he had left but the day before. There stood the Kaatskill Mountains — there ran the silver Hudson at a distance — there was every hill and dale precisely as it had always been. Rip was sorely perplexed. "That flagon last night," thought he, "has addled my poor head sadly!"

It was with some difficulty that he found the way to his own house, which he approached with silent awe, expecting every moment to hear the shrill voice of Dame Van Winkle. He found the house gone to decay — the roof fallen in, the windows shattered, and the doors off the hinges. A half-starved dog that looked like Wolf was skulking about it. Rip called him by name, but the cur snarled, showed his teeth, and passed on. This was an unkind cut indeed. "My very dog," sighed poor Rip, "has forgotten me!"

He entered the house, which, to tell the truth, Dame Van Winkle had always kept in neat order. It was empty, forlorn, and apparently abandoned. This desolateness overcame all his connubial fears — he called loudly for his wife and children; the lonely chambers rang for a moment with his voice, and then all again was silence.

He now hurried forth and hastened to his old resort, the village inn — but it too was gone. A large, rickety, wooden building stood in its place, with great gaping windows, some of them broken and mended

with old hats and petticoats, and over the door was painted, "the Union Hotel, by Jonathan Doolittle." Instead of the great tree that used to shelter the quiet little Dutch inn of yore, there now was reared a tall, naked pole, with something on the top that looked like a red nightcap, and from it was fluttering a flag, on which was a singular assemblage of stars and stripes — all this was strange and incomprehensible. He recognized on the sign, however, the ruby face of King George, under which he had smoked so many a peaceful pipe; but even this was singularly metamorphosed. The red coat was changed for one of blue and buff, a sword was held in the hand instead of a scepter, the head was decorated with a cocked hat, and underneath was painted in large characters, GENERAL WASHINGTON.

There was, as usual, a crowd of folk about the door, but none that Rip recollected. The very character of the people seemed changed. There was a busy, bustling, disputatious tone about it, instead of the accustomed phlegm and drowsy tranquility. He looked in vain for the sage Nicholas Vedder, with his broad face, double chin, and fair long pipe, uttering clouds of tobacco smoke instead of idle speeches; or Van Bummel, the schoolmaster, doling forth the contents of an ancient newspaper. In place of these, a lean, bilious-looking fellow, with his pockets full of handbills, was haranguing vehemently about rights of citizens — elections — members of congress — liberty — Bunker's Hill — heroes of seventy-six and other words, which were a perfect Babylonish jargon to the bewildered Van Winkle.

The appearance of Rip, with his long, grizzled beard, his rusty fowling piece, his uncouth dress, and an army of women and children at his heels, soon attracted the attention of the tavern politicians. They crowded around him, eyeing him from head to foot with great curiosity. The orator bustled up to him and, drawing him partly aside, inquired "on which side he voted?" Rip stared in vacant stupidity. Another short but busy little fellow pulled him by the arm, and, rising on tiptoe, inquired in his ear, "whether he was Federal or Democrat?" Rip was equally at a loss to comprehend the question; when a knowing, self-important old gentleman in a sharp cocked hat made his way through the crowd, putting them to the right and left with his elbows as he passed, and, planting himself before Van Winkle, with one arm akimbo, the other resting on his cane, his keen eyes and sharp hat penetrating, as it were, into his very soul, demanded in an austere tone, "what brought him to the election with a gun on his shoulder, and a mob at his heels, and whether he meant to breed a riot in the village?" "Alas! Gentlemen," cried Rip, somewhat dismayed, "I am a poor, quiet man, a native of the place, and a loyal subject of the king, God bless him!"

Here a general shout burst from the bystanders. "A tory! A tory! A spy! A refugee! Hustle him! Away with him!" It was with great difficulty that the self-important man in the cocked hat restored order; and, having assumed a tenfold austerity of brow, demanded again of the unknown culprit what he came there for and whom he was seeking. The poor man humbly assured him that he meant no harm, but merely came there in search of some of his neighbors, who used to keep about the tavern.

"Well — who are they? Name them."

Rip bethought himself a moment, and inquired, "Where's Nicholas Vedder?"

There was a silence for a little while, when an old man replied, in a thin, piping voice, "Nicholas Vedder! Why, he is dead and gone these eighteen years! There was a wooden tombstone in the churchyard that used to tell about him, but that's rotten and gone too."

"Where's Brom Dutcher?"

"Oh, he went off to the army in the beginning of the war; some say he was killed at the storming of Stony Point — others say he was drowned in a squall at the foot of Antony's Nose. I don't know — he never came back again."

"Where's Van Bummel, the schoolmaster?"

"He went off to the wars, too, was a great militia general, and is now in congress."

Rip's heart died away at hearing of these sad changes in his home and friends, and finding himself thus alone in the world. Every answer puzzled him, too, by treating of such enormous lapses of time and of matters which he could not understand: war — congress — Stony

Point. He had no courage to ask after any more friends, but cried out in despair, "Does nobody here know Rip Van Winkle?"

"Oh, Rip Van Winkle!" exclaimed two or three. "Oh, to be sure! That's Rip Van Winkle yonder, leaning against the tree."

Rip looked, and beheld a precise counterpart of himself as he went up the mountain: apparently as lazy, and certainly as ragged. The poor fellow was now completely confounded. He doubted his own identity, and whether he was himself or another man. In the midst of his bewilderment, the man in the cocked hat demanded who he was, and what was his name?

"God knows," exclaimed he, at his wit's end. "I'm not myself — I'm somebody else — that's me yonder — no — that's somebody else got into my shoes — I was myself last night, but I fell asleep on the mountain, and they've changed my gun, and everything's changed, and I'm changed, and I can't tell what's my name, or who I am!"

The bystanders began now to look at each other, nod, wink significantly, and tap their fingers against their foreheads. There was a whisper also about securing the gun and keeping the old fellow from doing mischief, at the very suggestion of which the self-important man in the cocked hat retired with some precipitation. At this critical moment a fresh, comely woman pressed through the throng to get a peep at the gray-bearded man. She had a chubby child in her arms, which, frightened at his looks, began to cry. "Hush, Rip," cried she, "hush, you little fool; the old man won't hurt you." The name of the child, the air of the mother, the tone of her voice, all awakened a train of recollections in his mind. "What is your name, my good woman?" asked he.

"Judith Gardenier."

"And your father's name?"

"Ah, poor man, Rip Van Winkle was his name, but it's twenty years since he went away from home with his gun, and never has been heard of since — his dog came home without him; but whether he shot himself, or was carried away by the Indians, nobody can tell. I was then but a little girl."

Rip had one question more to ask; but he put it in a faltering voice:

"Where's your mother?"

"Oh, she too had died but a short time since; she broke a blood vessel in a fit of passion, at a New England pedlar."

There was a drop of comfort, at least, in this intelligence. The honest man could contain himself no longer. He caught his daughter and her child in his arms. "I am your father!" cried he. "Young Rip Van Winkle once — old Rip Van Winkle now! Does nobody know poor Rip Van Winkle?"

All stood amazed, until an old woman, tottering out from among the crowd, put her hand to her brow and, peering under it in his face for a moment, exclaimed, "Sure enough! It is Rip Van Winkle — it is himself! Welcome home again, old neighbor. Why, where have you been these twenty long years?"

Rip's story was soon told, for the whole twenty years had been to him but as one night. The neighbors stared when they heard it; some were seen to wink at each other and put their tongues in their cheeks, and the self-important man in the cocked hat, who, when the alarm was over, had returned to the field, screwed down the corners of his mouth and shook his head — upon which there was a general shaking of the head throughout the assemblage.

It was determined, however, to take the opinion of old Peter Vanderdonk, who was seen slowly advancing up the road. He was a descendant of the historian of that name, who wrote one of the earliest accounts of the province. Peter was the most ancient inhabitant of the village, and well versed in all the wonderful events and traditions of the neighborhood. He recollected Rip at once and corroborated his story in the most satisfactory manner. He assured the company that it was a fact, handed down from his ancestor the historian, that the Kaatskill Mountains had always been haunted by strange beings. That it was affirmed that the great Hendrick Hudson, the first discoverer of the river and country, kept a kind of vigil there every twenty years, with his crew of the *Half Moon*, being permitted in this way to revisit the scenes of his enterprise and keep a guardian eye upon the river and the great city called by his name. That his father had once seen them in their old

Dutch dresses playing at ninepins in a hollow of the mountain, and that he himself had heard, one summer afternoon, the sound of their balls, like distant peals of thunder.

To make a long story short, the company broke up and returned to the more important concerns of the election. Rip's daughter took him home to live with her; she had a snug, well-furnished house, and a stout, cheery farmer for a husband, whom Rip recollected for one of the urchins that used to climb upon his back. As to Rip's son, and heir, who was the ditto of himself, seen leaning against the tree, he was employed to work on the farm, but evinced a hereditary disposition to attend to anything else but his business.

Rip now resumed his old walk and habits; he soon found many of his former cronies, though all rather the worse for the wear and tear of time, and preferred making friends among the rising generation, with whom he soon grew into great favor.

Having nothing to do at home, and being arrived at that happy age when a man can be idle with impunity, he took his place once more on the bench at the inn door and was reverenced as one of the patriarchs of the village, and a chronicle of the old times "before the war." It was some time before he could get into the regular track of gossip, or could be made to comprehend the strange events that had taken place during his torpor. How that there had been a revolutionary war — that the country had thrown off the yoke of old England — and that, instead of being a subject of his Majesty George the Third, he was now a free citizen of the United States. Rip, in fact, was no politician — the changes of states and empires made but little impression on him; but there was one species of despotism under which he had long groaned, and that was — petticoat government. Happily that was at an end; he had got his neck out of the yoke of matrimony and could go in and out whenever he pleased, without dreading the tyranny of Dame Van Winkle. Whenever her name was mentioned, however, he shook his head, shrugged his shoulders, and cast up his eyes, which might pass either for an expression of resignation to his fate or joy at his deliverance.

He used to tell his story to every stranger that arrived at Mr. Doolittle's hotel. He was observed, at first, to vary on some points every time he told it, which was, doubtless, owing to his having so recently awaked. It at last settled down precisely to the tale I have related, and not a man, woman, or child in the neighborhood but knew it by heart. Some always pretended to doubt the reality of it, and insisted that Rip had been out of his head, and that this was one point on which he always remained flighty. The old Dutch inhabitants, however, almost universally gave it full credit. Even to this day they never hear a thunderstorm of a summer afternoon about the Kaatskill but they say Hendrick Hudson and his crew are at their game of ninepins; and it is a common wish of all henpecked husbands in the neighborhood, when life hangs heavy on their hands, that they might have a quieting draft out of Rip Van Winkle's flagon.

ROSEMARY CARR AND
STEPHEN VINCENT BENÉT

NANCY HANKS
1784–1818

IF Nancy Hanks
Came back as a ghost,
Seeking news
Of what she loved most,
She'd ask first
"Where's my son?
What's happened to Abe?
What's he done?

"Poor little Abe,
Left all alone
Except for Tom,
Who's a rolling stone;
He was only nine
The year I died.
I remember still
How hard he cried.

"Scraping along
In a little shack,
With hardly a shirt
To cover his back,
And a prairie wind
To blow him down,
Or pinching times
If he went to town.

"You wouldn't know
About my son?
Did he grow tall?
Did he have fun?
Did he learn to read?
Did he get to town?
Did you know his name?
Did he get on?"

PECOS BILL

WELL now, the story goes that Pecos Bill was born in Tennessee, that being the farthest from anywhere that his parents could get. But one day Bill's ma noticed some new homesteaders about fifty miles away and she said to her family, "Family, it's time to move west. It's getting too crowded around here."

That very day they packed up their covered wagon and headed out to find some wide open spaces. They almost settled down in east Texas, but Bill's ma thought she spotted some branded cattle only a hundred miles away, so they kept on moving west.

As they crossed the Pecos River, Bill (being just a baby, you'll remember) fell right out the back of the wagon and into the rushing water. By the time his ma and pa and sisters and brothers noticed he wasn't in the back, they weren't quite sure just where they'd lost him. They all shed a tear, but Bill's ma said, "My kinfolk always know how to look after themselves. Bill will find us again one of these days. Now don't you fret."

Back at the river, Bill was doing his best to drink it dry. Just when he couldn't take another drop, a coyote snatched him out of the water by the scruff of the neck. She took him home with her

and raised him like one of her own pups in a den beside the river.

Years passed, and Bill grew and grew. He ran like a coyote. He howled like a coyote. He ate like a coyote. Some say he even thought like a coyote, but I don't know that for sure.

One day, Bill was sunning himself on a nice flat rock when a cowboy rode up and asked, "What are you doing out here in the middle of nowhere with nothing on?"

Bill laughed and said, "What do you mean what am I doing here? Why, I'm a coyote and this is what we do on a sunny day."

"You're no more coyote than I am," said the stranger, whose name was Joe. "You're almost a grown man and you're in Texas. Come along with me and I'll show it to you."

After Bill agreed to this plan, Joe lent him some clothes and gave him a new name — Pecos Bill. Then the two of them set off together into the mid-afternoon sun.

Bill and Joe had been traveling just a little ways when the biggest, meanest rattler in all Texas jumped out from behind a rock and wrapped itself around Bill's right leg. It was all ready to have that leg for an afternoon snack when Bill reached down and grabbed the snake behind the jaws and began to squeeze.

Now you might find this hard to believe, but Bill wrung that rattler out like a wet towel till there wasn't a drop of poison left in it. The rattler put up the best fight it could, because there's nothing more embarrassing for a snake than being used like a common house towel. Finally, though, he had to hiss, "OK, OK, you win. Just straighten me out and I'll come with you."

So Bill coiled the rattler like a good piece of rope and slung him over his shoulder, and he and Joe continued their sightseeing.

A few days later they were moseying down a gulch, minding their own business, when they were attacked by a horrible monster. It was part 'gator, part cougar and part armadillo. It was green and mean and had the longest claws you ever saw. Bill and the monster wrestled till the dust they raised in the dry gulch blocked out the sun. There was so much dust, they didn't even notice when day turned into night. And they didn't notice when their wrestling turned that little dry gulch into the decade's worst duststorm.

Now, Bill decided he was downright tired of all that dust. He wrestled that monster into giving him a ride on his back, and by the time they'd run the length of Texas and back, they were friends for life.

Eventually, Bill and Joe and the snake and the monster stumbled into the canyon where the outlaws of the Hell's Gulch Gang were hiding out. They were the toughest, fiercest cattle rustlers in the whole state. But they took one look at their visitors and hid behind their horses.

"Who's boss of this here outfit?" Bill called out.

"I was," said their leader Gun Smith. "But I reckon you is now."

Bill decided that the gang wasn't really bad. They were just bored and frustrated and it made them mean. You see, to catch a longhorn, they had to set a circle of wire like a rabbit snare on the ground and wait till a steer was stupid enough to walk into it. Then they'd draw the wire tight and trip the animal. As you can imagine, it took a long time to rustle cattle that way.

Despite his unusual upbringing, Bill was a law-abiding sort, so he made the gang promise that they would only rustle stray steer with no brands. And then he tied a noose in one end of his snake and sailed it through the air till it landed around the neck of an unsuspecting long-horn. Now that animal was scared right out of its wits with a rattler looped around its neck. It bucked and kicked to get out of that noose, but nothing worked. Finally, it got scared right out of its skin and ran off to grow another.

Bill had just invented the very first lasso.

Soon the Hell's Gulch Gang had rounded up so many cattle that they realized they were going to need a big ranch to go with them. Bill, liked the looks of Pinnacle Peak and they all settled there.

But soon the gang began getting mean again. They were tired of herding the cattle from January to December. Yup, they were getting as mean as Bill's monster, and Bill knew he had to do something about it. So he set up twenty gophers in a row and as quick as they could dig a hole, Bill slipped in a fence post. Now this made the gophers pretty darn mad and they kept running to the head of the line and digging new holes. They never did figure out that that was just what Bill wanted. In no time at all, Bill had his range around Pinnacle Peak all fenced off so that his gang didn't have to work so hard.

If the steers felt like a little winter grazing, they climbed to the top of the peak. If they felt like summer grass, why they just came down again. No more endless driving from the winter to the summer ranges. The only thing the gang had to do was rescue the odd cow or steer that fell off a steep bit of mountain.

The Pinnacle Peak Ranch cowboys were happy once more, but Bill wasn't. Joe, who's still in this story, took him aside and said, "Bill, you're the greatest cowboy Texas has ever seen. You need the greatest horse. That will fix what ails you."

And so saying, he sent Bill off to find Lightning, the wildest, fastest, most beautiful mustang in the land. Now, this might surprise you, but in the beginning Lightning declined the privilege of being tamed by Pecos Bill and took off like a prairie summer storm.

Bill tracked him across three states to the Rocky Mountains and back four to the Great Smokies. He followed him north to the Tombstone Range and south to the Andes. (This horse had a thing for mountains.)

Finally, somewhere around the Mexican–American border, Lightning got tired. Actually, Bill was pretty bushed, too. He caught up to the horse, though, and sang to him in the language of the animals he had learned from the coyotes. They tell me it was pretty poetical but it basically boiled down to "I'm the greatest cowboy there ever was and you're the greatest horse, so let's team up."

Lightning agreed. Together they decided they'd had enough of touring the continents for now and started back to the ranch. They were about to cross the Pecos River again, when Slewfoot Sue rode by on the back of a Texas catfish.

It was love at first sight. Bill knew she was the only woman for him and immediately asked her to marry him. Slewfoot Sue replied, "It sounds like an OK idea to me but I've got two conditions. First, you've

got to buy me one of those fancy weddin' dresses with the bustles. And then, you've got to let me ride Lightning."

The first condition was easy. Bill and Lightning took off to San Anton' to buy the dress. It took them half an hour because the store clerk was busy. As soon as they got back, Slewfoot Sue tried on her new dress and said it was the fanciest she'd ever seen.

Bill was a little nervous about the second condition. Lightning didn't let just anybody ride him. But the horse and Sue got along just fine. The only thing was, Sue got real excited and decided to do a fancy slide off Lightning's back. She landed on her bustle, which acted just like a giant spring and sent her off as high as Pinnacle Peak. On her second bounce, she went as high as the moon. On her third, she discovered Mars.

Each time she came back to earth, Bill tried to catch her. For three days and three nights, Slewfoot Sue bounced. Bill was getting desperate. It was supposed to be his wedding day, after all. On the first bounce of the fourth day, Bill thought he was going to lose her for sure. With a last throw of his lasso, he caught her as she touched down, but darned if she didn't bounce up again and if Bill didn't get hauled up with her.

But Bill was Pecos Bill after all, and he lassoed them both to a passing tornado and they rode it all the way out to California. As the tornado wound down, Bill realized they were going to crash-land in somebody's covered wagon.

They slammed through the canvas top and dropped right into two empty chairs set at the table inside. Bill's ma looked up from carving a roast and said, "Hello, Bill. You still like two helpings?"

You see, Bill's ma never did find the right empty spot to settle down on, and they were still wandering the land. Bill told her that she'd passed right on by the best place and that the family should come back with him to Texas.

So they all returned to Texas where Bill's adventures never stopped and where he and Slewfoot Sue had lots of kids and lived happily ever after.

LAURA INGALLS WILDER

CAP GARLAND

The Ingalls family had always lived far out on the prairies or deep in the woods. But now Ma is determined to send her girls to school, so they have settled in a new frontier town in the Dakota Territory. Mary, the oldest daughter, is blind and must study at home. In this excerpt from The Long Winter, *her sisters, Laura and Carrie, are anxiously anticipating their first day of school.*

 AURA did not sleep very well. All night, it seemed, she knew that the town was close around her and that she must go to school in the morning. She was heavy with dread when she woke and heard steps going by in the street below and strange men speaking. The town was waking up too; the storekeepers were opening their stores.

The walls of the house kept strangers outside. But Laura and Carrie were heavyhearted because they must go out of the house and meet strangers. And Mary was sad because she could not go to school.

"Now Laura and Carrie, there's no cause to worry," Ma said. "I'm sure you can keep up with your classes."

They looked at Ma in surprise. She had taught them so well at home that they knew they could keep up with their classes. They were not worried about that. But they only said, "Yes, Ma."

They hurried to wash the dishes and make their bed and hurriedly Laura swept their bedroom floor. Then they dressed carefully in their woolen winter dresses and nervously combed their hair and braided it. They tied on their Sunday hair-ribbons. With the steel buttonhook they buttoned their shoes.

"Hurry up, girls!" Ma called. "It's past eight o'clock."

At that moment, Carrie nervously jerked one of her shoe-buttons off. It fell and rolled and vanished down a crack of the floor.

"Oh, it's gone!" Carrie gasped. She was desperate. She could not go where strangers would see that gap in the row of black buttons that buttoned up her shoe.

"We must take a button off one of Mary's shoes," Laura said.

But Ma had heard the button fall, downstairs. She found it and sewed it on again, and buttoned the shoe for Carrie.

At last they were ready. "You look very nice," Ma said, smiling. They put on their coats and hoods and took their schoolbooks. They said good-bye to Ma and Mary and they went out into Main Street.

The stores were all open. Mr. Fuller and Mr. Bradley had finished sweeping out; they stood holding their brooms and looking at the morning. Carrie took hold of Laura's hand. It helped Laura, to know that Carrie was even more scared than she was.

Bravely they crossed wide Main Street and walked steadily on along Second Street. The sun was shining brightly. A tangle of dead weeds and grasses made shadows beside the wheel-tracks. Their own long shadows went before them, over many footprints in the paths. It seemed a long, long way to the schoolhouse that stood on the open prairie with no other buildings near.

In front of the schoolhouse strange boys were playing ball, and two strange girls stood on the platform before the entry door.

Laura and Carrie came nearer and nearer. Laura's throat was so choked that she could hardly breathe. One of the strange girls was tall and dark. Her smooth, black hair was twisted into a heavy knot at the back of her head. Her dress of indigo blue woolen was longer than Laura's brown one.

Then suddenly Laura saw one of the boys spring into the air and catch the ball. He was tall and quick and he moved as beautifully as a cat. His yellow hair was sun-bleached almost white and his eyes were blue. They saw Laura and opened wide. Then a flashing grin lighted up his whole face and he threw the ball to her.

She saw the ball curving down through the air, coming swiftly. Before she could think, she had made a running leap and caught it.

A great shout went up from the other boys. "Hey, Cap!" they shouted. "Girls don't play ball!"

"I didn't think she'd catch it," Cap answered.

"I don't want to play," Laura said. She threw back the ball.

"She's as good as any of us!" Cap shouted. "Come on and play," he said to Laura, and then to the other girls, "Come on, Mary Power and Minnie! You play with us, too!"

But Laura picked up the books she had dropped and took Carrie's hand again. They went on to the other girls at the schoolhouse door. Those girls would not play with boys, of course. She did not know why she had done such a thing and she was ashamed, fearful of what those girls must be thinking of her.

"I'm Mary Power," the dark girl said, "and this is Minnie Johnson." Minnie Johnson was thin and fair and pale, with freckles.

"I'm Laura Ingalls," Laura said, "and this is my little sister, Carrie."

Mary Power's eyes smiled. They were dark blue eyes, fringed with long, black lashes. Laura smiled back and she made up her mind that she would twist up her own hair tomorrow and ask Ma to make her next dress as long as Mary's.

"That was Cap Garland that threw you the ball," Mary Power said.

There was no time to say anything more, for the teacher came to the door with the hand-bell, and they all went in to school.

They hung their coats and hoods on a row of nails in the entry, where the broom stood in a corner by the water-pail on its bench. Then they went into the school-room.

It was so new and shining that Laura felt timid again, and Carrie stood close to her. All the desks were patent desks, made of wood varnished as smooth as glass. They had black iron feet and the seats were curved a little, with curving backs that were part of the desks behind them. The desk-tops had grooves to hold pencils and shelves underneath them for slates and books.

There were twelve of these desks in a row up each side of the big room. A large heating stove stood in the middle of the room, with four more desks in front of it and four more behind it. Almost all those seats were empty. On the girls' side of the room, Mary Power and Minnie Johnson sat together in one of the back seats. Cap Garland and three other big boys sat in back seats on the boys' side — a few little boys and girls sat in front seats. They had all been coming to school, for a week now, and knew where to sit, but Laura and Carrie did not.

The teacher said to them, "You're new, aren't you?" She was a smiling young lady, with curled bangs. The bodice of her black dress was buttoned down the front with twinkling jet buttons. Laura told her their names and she said, "And I'm Florence Garland. We live back of your father's place, on the next street."

So Cap Garland was Teacher's brother and they lived in the new house out on the prairie beyond the stable.

"Do you know the Fourth Reader?" Teacher asked.

"Oh, yes, ma'am!" Laura said. She did indeed know every word of it.

"Then I think we'll see what you can do with the Fifth," Teacher decided. And she told Laura to take the back seat in the middle row, across the aisle from Mary Power. Carrie she put in front, near the little girls, and then she went up to her desk and rapped on it with her ruler.

"The school will come to attention," she said. She opened her Bible. "This morning I will read the twenty-third Psalm."

Laura knew the Psalms by heart, of course, but she loved to hear again every word of the twenty-third, from " 'The Lord is my shepherd: I shall not want,' " to, " 'Surely goodness and mercy shall follow me all the days of my life: and I will dwell in the house of the Lord forever.' "

Then Teacher closed the Bible and on all the desks the pupils opened their textbooks. School work had begun.

Every day Laura liked the school more. She had no seat-mate, but at recess and noontimes she was with Mary Power and Minnie Johnson. After school they walked to Main Street together, and by the end of that week they were meeting in the mornings and walking together to school. Twice Cap Garland urged them to play ball with the boys at recess, but they stayed inside the schoolhouse and watched the game through the window.

The brown-eyed, dark-haired boy was Ben Woodworth who lived at the depot. His father was the sick man that Pa had sent out with the last teamster the year before. The "prairie cure" had truly almost cured his consumption of the lungs and he had come West again for more for it. He was the depot agent now.

The other boy was Arthur Johnson. He was thin and fair like his sister Minnie. Cap Garland was strongest and quickest. Inside the window, Laura and Mary and Minnie all watched him throwing the ball and leaping to catch it. He was not as handsome as black-haired Ben, but there was something about him. He was always good-natured and his grin was like a flash of light. It was like the sun coming up at dawn; it changed everything.

Mary Power and Minnie had gone to schools in the East, but Laura found it easy to keep up with them in their lessons. Cap Garland was from the East, too, but even in arithmetic he could not beat Laura.

Every night after supper she put her books and her slate on the red-checkered tablecloth in the lamplight, and she studied next day's lessons with Mary. She read the arithmetic problems aloud, and Mary did them in her head while she worked them on the slate. She read the history lesson and the geography to Mary until both of them could answer every question. If ever Pa could get money enough to send Mary to the college for the blind, Mary must be ready to go.

"And even if I never can go to college," Mary said, "I am learning as much as I can."

Mary and Laura and Carrie were all enjoying school so much that they were sorry when Saturday and Sunday interrupted it. They looked forward to Monday. But when Monday came Laura was cross because her red flannel underwear was so hot and scratchy.

It made her back itch, and her neck, and her wrists, and where it was folded around her ankles, under her stockings and shoe-tops, that red flannel almost drove her crazy.

At noon she begged Ma to let her change to cooler underthings. "It's too hot for my red flannels, Ma!" she protested.

"I know the weather's turned warm," Ma answered gently. "But this is the time of year to wear flannels, and you would catch cold if you took them off."

Laura went crossly back to school and sat squirming because she must not scratch. She held the flat geography open before her, but she wasn't studying. She was trying to bear the itching flannels and wanting to get home where she could scratch. The sunshine from the western windows had never crawled so slowly.

Suddenly there was no sunshine. It went out, as if someone had blown out the sun like a lamp. The outdoors was gray, the windowpanes were gray, and at the same moment a wind crashed against the school-house, rattling windows and doors and shaking walls.

Miss Garland started up from her chair. One of the little Beardsley girls screamed and Carrie turned white.

Laura thought, "It happened this way on Plum Creek, the Christmas when Pa was lost." Her whole heart hoped and prayed that Pa was safe at home now.

Teacher and all the others were staring at the windows, where nothing but grayness could be seen. They all looked frightened. Then Miss Garland said, "It is only a storm, children. Go on with your lessons."

The blizzard was scouring against the walls, and the winds squealed and moaned in the stovepipe.

All the heads bent over the books as Teacher had told them to do. But Laura was trying to think how to get home. The schoolhouse was a long way from Main Street, and there was nothing to guide them.

All the others had come from the East that summer. They had never seen a prairie blizzard. But Laura and Carrie knew what it was. Carrie's head was bowed limply above her book, and the back of it, with the white parting between the braids of fine, soft hair, looked small and helpless and frightened.

There was only a little fuel at the schoolhouse. The school board was buying coal, but only one load had been delivered. Laura thought they might outlive the storm in the schoolhouse, but they could not do it without burning all the costly patent desks.

Without lifting her head Laura looked up at Teacher. Miss Garland was thinking and biting her lip. She could not decide to dismiss school because of a storm, but this storm frightened her.

"I ought to tell her what to do," Laura thought. But she could not think what to do. It was not safe to leave the schoolhouse and it was not safe to stay there. Even the twelve patent desks might not last long enough to keep them warm until the blizzard ended. She thought of her wraps and Carrie's, in the entry. Whatever happened she must somehow keep Carrie warm. Already the cold was coming in.

There was a loud thumping in the entry. Every pupil started and looked at the door.

It opened and a man stumbled in. He was bundled in overcoat, cap, and muffler, all solid white with snow driven into the woolen cloth. They could not see who he was until he pulled down the stiffened muffler.

"I came out to get you," he told Teacher.

He was Mr. Foster, the man who owned the ox team and had come in from his claim to stay in town for the winter at Sherwood's, across the street from Teacher's house.

Miss Garland thanked him. She rapped her ruler on the desk and said, "Attention! School is dismissed. You may bring your wraps from the entry and put them on by the stove."

Laura said to Carrie, "You stay here. I'll bring your wraps."

The entry was freezing cold, snow was blowing in between the rough boards of the walls. Laura was chilled before she could snatch her coat and hood from their nail. She found Carrie's and carried the armful into the schoolhouse.

Crowded around the stove, they all put on their wraps and fastened them snugly. Cap Garland did not smile. His blue eyes narrowed and his mouth set straight while Mr. Foster talked.

Laura wrapped the muffler snugly over Carrie's white face and took firm hold of her mittened hand. She told Carrie, "Don't worry, we'll be all right."

"Now, just follow me," said Mr. Foster, taking Teacher's arm. "And keep close together."

He opened the door, led the way with Miss Garland. Mary Power and Minnie each took one of the little Beardsley girls. Ben and Arthur followed them closely, then Laura went out with Carrie into the blinding snow. Cap shut the door behind them.

They could hardly walk in the beating, whirling wind. The school-house had disappeared. They could see nothing but swirling whiteness and snow and then a glimpse of each other, disappearing like shadows.

Laura felt that she was smothering. The icy particles of snow whirled scratching into her eyes and smothered her breathing. Her skirts whipped around her, now wrapped so tightly that she could not step, then whirled and lifted to her knees. Suddenly tightening, they made her stumble. She held tightly to Carrie, and Carrie, struggling and staggering, was pulled away by the wind and then flung back against her.

"We can't go on this way," Laura thought. But they had to.

She was alone in the confusion of whirling winds and snow except for Carrie's hand that she must never let go. The winds struck her this way and that. She could not see nor breathe, she stumbled and was falling, then suddenly she seemed to be lifted and Carrie bumped against her. She tried to think. The others must be somewhere ahead. She must walk faster and keep up with them or she and Carrie would be lost. If they were lost on the prairie they would freeze to death.

But perhaps they were all lost. Main Street was only two blocks long. If they were going only a little way to north or south they would miss the block of stores and beyond was empty prairie for miles.

Laura thought they must have gone far enough to reach Main Street, but she could see nothing.

The storm thinned a little. She saw shadowy figures ahead. They were darker gray in the whirling gray-whiteness. She went on as fast as she could, with Carrie, until she touched Miss Garland's coat.

They had all stopped. Huddled in their wraps, they stood like bundles close together in the swirling mist. Teacher and Mr. Foster were trying to talk, but the winds confused their shouts so that no one could hear what they said. Then Laura began to know how cold she was.

Her mittened hand was so numb that it hardly felt Carrie's hand. She was shaking all over and deep inside her there was a shaking that she could not stop. Only in her very middle there was a solid knot that ached, and her shaking pulled this knot tighter so that the ache grew worse.

She was frightened about Carrie. The cold hurt too much, Carrie could not stand it. Carrie was so little and thin, she had always been delicate, she could not stand such cold much longer. They must reach shelter soon.

Mr. Foster and Teacher were moving again, going a little to the left. All the others stirred and hurried to follow them. Laura took hold of Carrie with her other hand, that had been in her coat pocket and was not quite so numb, and then suddenly she saw a shadow go by them. She knew it was Cap Garland.

He was not following the others to the left. With hands in his pockets and head bent, he went trudging straight ahead into the storm. A fury of winds thickened the air with snow and he vanished.

Laura did not dare follow him. She must take care of Carrie and Teacher had told them to follow her. She was sure that Cap was going toward Main Street, but perhaps she was mistaken and she could not take Carrie away from the others.

She kept tight told of Carrie and hurried to follow Mr. Foster and Teacher as fast as she could. Her chest sobbed for air and her eyes strained open in the icy snow-particles that hurt them like sand. Carrie struggled bravely, stumbling and flopping, doing her best to stay on her feet and keep on going. Only for instants when the snow-whirl was thinner could they glimpse the shadows moving ahead of them.

Laura felt that they were going in the wrong direction. She did not know why she felt so. No one could see anything. There was nothing to go by — no sun, no sky, no direction in the winds blowing fiercely from all directions. There was nothing but the dizzy whirling and the cold.

It seemed that the cold and the winds, the noise of the winds and the blinding, smothering, scratching snow, and the effort and the aching, were forever. Pa had lived through three days of a blizzard under the bank of Plum Creek. But there were no creek banks here. Here there was nothing but bare prairie. Pa had told about sheep caught in a blizzard, huddled together under the snow. Some of them had lived. Perhaps people could do that, too. Carrie was too tired to go much farther, but she was too heavy for Laura to carry. They must go on as long as they could, and then . . .

Then, out of the whirling whiteness, something hit her. The hard blow crashed against her shoulder and all through her. She rocked on her feet and stumbled against something solid. It was high, it was hard, it was the corner of two walls. Her hands felt it, her eyes saw it. She had walked against some building.

With all her might she yelled, "Here! Come here! Here's a house!"

All around the house the winds were howling so that at first no one heard her. She pulled the icy stiff muffler from her mouth and screamed into the blinding storm. At last she saw a shadow in it, two tall shadows thinner than the shadowy wall she clung to — Mr. Foster and Teacher. Then other shadows pressed close around her.

No one tried to say anything. They crowded together and they were all there — Mary Power and Minnie, each with a little Beardsley girl, and Arthur Johnson and Ben Woodworth with the small Wilmarth boys. Only Cap Garland was missing.

They followed along the side of that building till they came to the front of it, and it was Mead's Hotel, at the very north end of Main Street.

Beyond it was nothing but the railroad track covered with snow, the lonely depot and the wide, open prairie. If Laura had been only a few steps nearer the others, they would all have been lost on the endless prairie north of town.

For a moment they stood by the hotel's lamplit windows. Warmth and rest were inside the hotel, but the blizzard was growing worse and they must all reach home.

Main Street would guide all of them except Ben Woodworth. No other buildings stood between the hotel and the depot where he lived. So Ben went into the hotel to stay till the blizzard was over. He could afford to do that because his father had a regular job.

Minnie and Arthur Johnson, taking the little Wilmarth boys, had only to cross Main Street to Wilmarth's grocery store and their home was beside it. The others went on down Main Street, keeping close to the buildings. They passed the saloon, they passed Royal Wilder's feed store, and then they passed Barker's grocery. The Beardsley Hotel was next and there the little Beardsley girls went in.

The journey was almost ended now. They passed Couse's Hardware store and they crossed Second Street to Fuller's Hardware. Mary Power had only to pass the drugstore now. Her father's tailor shop stood next to it.

Laura and Carrie and Teacher and Mr. Foster had to cross Main Street now. It was a wide street. But if they missed Pa's house, the haystacks and the stable were still between them and the open prairie.

They did not miss the house. One of its lighted windows made a glow that Mr. Foster saw before he ran into it. He went on around the house corner with Teacher to go by the clothesline, the haystacks, and the stable to the Garland house.

Laura and Carrie were safe at their own front door. Laura's hands fumbled at the doorknob, too stiff to turn it. Pa opened the door and helped them in.

He was wearing overcoat and cap and muffler. He had set down the lighted lantern and dropped a coil of rope. "I was just starting out after you," he said.

In the still house Laura and Carrie stood taking deep breaths. It was so quiet there where the winds did not push and pull at them. They were still blinded, but the whirling icy snow had stopped hurting their eyes.

Laura felt Ma's hands breaking away the icy muffler, and she said, "Is Carrie all right?"

"Yes, Carrie's all right," said Pa.

Ma took off Laura's hood and unbuttoned her coat and helped her pull out of its sleeves. "These wraps are driven full of ice," Ma said. They crackled when she shook them and little drifts of whiteness sifted to the floor.

"Well," Ma said, " 'All's well that ends well.' You're not frostbitten. You can go to the fire and get warm."

Laura could hardly move but she stooped and with her fingers dug out the caked snow that the wind had driven in between her woolen stockings and the tops of her shoes. Then she staggered toward the stove.

"Take my place," Mary said, getting up from her rocking chair. "It's the warmest."

Laura sat stiffly down. She felt numb and stupid. She rubbed her eyes and saw a pink smear on her hand. Her eyelids were bleeding where the snow had scratched them. The sides of the coal heater glowed red-hot and she could feel the heat on her skin, but she was cold inside. The heat from the fire couldn't reach that cold.

Pa sat close to the stove holding Carrie on his knee. He had taken off her shoes to make sure that her feet were not frozen and he held her wrapped in a shawl. The shawl shivered with Carrie's shivering. "I can't get warm, Pa," she said.

"You girls are chilled through. I'll have you a hot drink in a minute," said Ma, hurrying into the kitchen.

She brought them each a steaming cup of ginger tea.

"My, that smells good!" said Mary and Grace leaned on Laura's knee looking longingly at the cup till Laura gave her a sip and Pa said, "I don't know why there's not enough of that to go around."

"Maybe there is," said Ma, going into the kitchen again.

It was so wonderful to be there, safe at home, sheltered from the winds and the cold. Laura thought that this must be a little bit like Heaven, where the weary are at rest. She could not imagine that Heaven was better than being where she was, slowly growing warm and comfortable, sipping the hot, sweet, ginger tea, seeing Ma, and Grace, and Pa and Carrie, and Mary all enjoying their own cups of it and hearing the storm that could not touch them here.

"I'm glad you didn't have to come for us, Pa," Laura said drowsily. "I was hoping you were safe."

"So was I," Carrie told Pa, snuggling against him. "I remembered that Christmas, on Plum Creek, when you didn't get home."

"I did, too," Pa said grimly. "When Cap Garland came into Fuller's and said you were all heading out to the open prairie, you can bet I made tracks for a rope and lantern."

"I'm glad we got in all right," Laura woke up to say.

"Yes, we'd have had a posse out looking for you, though we'd have been hunting for a needle in a haystack," said Pa.

"Best forget about it," said Ma.

"Well, he did the best he could," Pa went on. "Cap Garland's a smart boy."

"And now, Laura and Carrie, you're going to bed and get some rest," said Ma. "A good long sleep is what you need."

JACK AND THE NORTH WEST WIND

NE time Jack and his folks lived in an old rickety house on top of a hill, and this time I'm tellin' you about, Jack and his mother were the only ones at home. Jack's daddy was off somewhere on the public works a-buildin' road, and Jack's two brothers, Will and Tom, they'd gone off to another settlement huntin' 'em a job of work.

Well, winter came and directly the weather got awful bad. It turned off real cold and set in to snowin' and then the North West Wind commenced to blow, and one day hit got to whistlin' in through the cracks of that old house, and Jack and his mother nearly froze.

Jack's mother told him he ought to get some boards and fix up the house a little. Jack studied awhile over that, and he recollected that Will had broke the hammer crackin' walnuts, and Tom had used up all the nails mendin' the fence, and that there wasn't any boards except a few old rotten pieces at the barn. So Jack told his mother, No, said what he'd do, if it was him, he'd go and stop that North West Wind so it wouldn't blow.

His mother asked him how in the world he could do that, and Jack told her he'd go find the place where the wind came out, take his old hat and plug it right in the hole.

Jack's mother told him, says, "Why, Jack, you know that can't be done."

But Jack said that was the very thing he aimed to do — said he could try it anyhow.

So Jack spent pretty near all one day splittin' his mother a big enough pile of firewood to do her till he got back. Then real early the next morning he got his old raggedy hat and pulled out.

He traveled on, traveled on, traveled on, till he got a right far ways from home, and just 'fore dark he met up with an old man with a long gray beard.

He was standin' there one side of the road, and when Jack got up to him, seemed like he knowed Jack, says, "Hello, Jack! What you up to this cold winter day?"

"I've started out to stop that North West Wind," says Jack. "We're just about to freeze to death back home."

"Why, Jack, you can't stop the North West Wind."

"Oh, yes, I can!" says Jack. "I'll stop it all right — just as soon as I find the hole where it comes out at."

"That might be an awful long way off, Jack," says the old man. "You just better come on up and stay the night with me."

"Much obliged," says Jack, "but I reckon I better keep goin'. Just come and go with me."

"Why, I can't let you stay out on the road, Jack. There ain't another house between here and the state line. You come on home with me and we'll have us a snack to eat and talk this thing over 'fore ye go any further."

Well, Jack was pretty hungry, so he went on home with the old man, and they fixed up a good dinner, and Jack didn't have to be begged to sit down at the table. They got done eatin' directly and Jack helped get the dishes washed up. Then the old man says to Jack, says, "Now, Jack, you ought to go on back home tonight and look after your mother. If you do that, I'll give ye a nice present. I've got a tablecloth here and all you have to do is lay it out and say,

'Spread, tablecloth! Spread!'

and ever'thing'll come on it that anybody'd want to eat."

"All right," says Jack. "That would be a mighty nice thing to have. We ain't got much to eat just now, anyway."

So the old man wrapped up that tablecloth ready for Jack to start, says, "Now, Jack, you be sure and not stop at this next house back down the road. There's some awful rowdy boys live there, and if you hang around 'em much, they're liable to steal your tablecloth."

Well, Jack thanked the old man and took his tablecloth and went on.

He came to that house and those boys happened to be out in the yard. They came out in the road and started talkin' to Jack and Jack played with 'em awhile, and then they begged Jack to stop and lay up with 'em that night. It was gettin' 'way along late in the evenin', so Jack he went on in, and directly the boys got to askin' him why he had that tablecloth under his arm. Jack didn't tell 'em at first, but they got to pesterin' him and teasin' him so that finally Jack told 'em. They wouldn't believe him and started makin' fun of him till Jack unrolled it, said,

"Spread, tablecloth! Spread!"

And all manner of good vittles came out on it. So they all sat down and eat a big supper. Then Jack rolled it back up.

Well, that night after Jack was asleep, the boys took another table-cloth and put it in the place of Jack's. And the next morning Jack was up early and got back in home.

He came on in the house, his mother says, "Well, Jack, ye never stopped that Wind. Hit's a-blowin' right on."

"No," says Jack, "I never got to the place where it come out at. An old man gave me a present to come on back home."

"What did he give ye, Jack?"

So Jack told her about the tablecloth and what it could do.

"You try it out, then," his mother says. "I sure would like to see that."

Jack laid it out, says,

"Spread, tablecloth! Spread!"

But there didn't ever a thing come on it.

So Jack's mother took his tablecloth and cut it up. Made him a shirt out of it.

II

Jack stayed on at home about a week, and then that North West Wind got to blowin' hard again. So one day Jack told his mother, says, "I'm a-goin' to try again about stoppin' that wind, now, and you needn't look for me back till I get it stopped."

So Jack got his mother up a big pile of firewood and pulled out again. Took the same route he took before, and when he came to where that old man lived, Jack slipped through a field so he wouldn't be seen. Got back in the road and went on. He came to a mill after a while, and there was the old man just comin' out with his turn of meal on his shoulder, says, "Hello, Jack! Where you started to again this cold day?"

"I'm a-goin' to stop that North West Wind, uncle," says Jack, "and I'm goin' on this time till I get it plumb stopped."

"Why you'll freeze to death 'fore ye get to where that Wind comes out, Jack. You better just turn around and come on back up to the house with me."

"I ain't goin' to fool with you," says Jack. "That old tablecloth you gave me wouldn't do what you said it would."

"Did you stop at that house where I told ye not to stop at?"

"Yes. I stayed the night there."

"They've got your tablecloth, Jack. You just go on home with me now, and I'll see if I haven't got somethin' else to give ye. We'll build us up a good warm fire and fix a little somethin' to eat too."

Well, Jack was gettin' pretty cold and he was hungry, so he went on up with the old man and they got dinner fixed. After they got through eating and got the dishes washed, the old man let Jack sit by his fire till he got good and warm, then he says to him, says, "Now, Jack, I'm goin' to give ye a rooster to take home and all you have to do is hold your hat under it and say,

'Come, gold! Come!'

and that rooster'll lay your hat full of golden eggs."

So Jack put the rooster under his arm and thanked the old man, and pulled out for home. The old man hollered after him, says, "You recollect now and not stop at that place where them devilish boys are."

Jack hollered back and said All right.

He went on and got past that house, but he met up with the boys in the road. First thing, they began to ask him what the old man gave him that time, and finally Jack had to tell 'em, and they said there couldn't no rooster lay eggs at all, let alone gold ones. Said Jack was makin' up a whopper. So Jack set the rooster down and took his hat, says,

"Come, gold! Come!"

and the gold just came a-pourin' out.

Then the boys said to him, says, "Why, Jack, you've just got to stay all night with us. You sure ought to show that trick to daddy when he comes in."

Well, they talked so good that finally Jack decided to stay. The boys' father took on a sight when they showed him about that rooster and he got Jack a box to keep it in that night. Jack slept hard and didn't wake up at all when the boys slipped in his room and took his rooster out of the box and put another one in the place of it. It was so near like the real one that Jack didn't notice it when he took it out the next morning and went on back in home.

When he got there, his mother said to him, says, "Well, Jack, I see you're back, and that Wind's a-blowin' right on."

"I never found the place where it comes out at, yet," says Jack. "Saw that old man again, and he hired me to come back."

"What did he give ye this time?"

Jack told her about his rooster, and she told him, says, "Let me see now whether it will or not."

Jack set the rooster out, says,

"Come, gold! Come!"

but there wasn't a single egg to come. The old rooster just jumped up on a chair and crowed right big.

"Hit's a failure, Jack. You made a bobble this time, too."

So they killed the rooster and eat it for supper.

III

Jack stayed around home several days and tended to his feedin' and milkin' and kept up a good pile of wood by the fire; and then that North West Wind started blowin' the hardest yet. It blasted right on through the house and whistled around the chimney and it commenced snowin' in all over everything. Looked like a regular harricane was comin'. Blew through that old open house so hard it nearly put the fire out. Fin'ly Jack says to his mother, says, "I'm bound to go stop that Wind." Says, "And that old man ain't a-goin' to turn me back this time either. We'll freeze to death if that Wind ain't stopped."

Well, Jack worked hard gettin' up enough wood to do his mother a long time, and then he pulled out again. When he got near that old man's place, he cut out through the woods so he couldn't see him at all.

But he hadn't gone any piece at all hardly 'fore he came on the old man out there a-rabbit huntin', says, "Hel-lo, Jack! What in the world you doin' back here again?"

"I'm goin' to stop that North West Wind," says Jack, "and I'm a-goin' on this time, too!"

"What did ye do with the rooster I give ye, Jack?"

"Hit wouldn't do a thing you said. We killed it and eat it."

"Did you stop at that house again, Jack?"

"Yes," says Jack. "I stayed the night there."

"They've got your rooster. That's what happened sure." Says, "Now, Jack, you better just leave that North West Wind alone now and come on home with me again. We'll have to talk this over and see what we can do. No *Sir!* I'll not let you go no further this cold stormy day."

Well, Jack was pretty near give out with stumblin' through the snow, and he was cold and hungry too, so he let the old man have his way. They fixed up a good dinner, and Jack sat by the fire and got good and warm and rested, and directly the old man reached up over the fire-board and got down a little knotty-lookin' club, says, "If you go back this time, Jack, I'll give ye this club."

And he handed it to Jack, says, "Now, you can just take the club and say,

'Playaway, club! Playaway!'

and it'll do any knockin' you want done. Hit'll even knock up wood for ye." Says, "And this time I'm a-goin' to show ye it'll do what I tell ye, 'fore you leave."

So he took Jack outside the door and told Jack to tell it —

"Playaway, club! Playaway!
Knock up some wood!"

So Jack told it and hit went and knocked down a big tree, knocked it right down off the hill plumb into the yard, knocked it into firewood, and broke some of it up into kindlin'.

Jack just laughed and slapped his hands together, says, "I'll sure go home! That's the very thing I been a-wantin'!"

So he got the club, and told the old man he was much obliged and started on back home. The old man came out and hollered after him, says, "Now, you be sure and not stop at that house where them rowdy boys are."

"No. I'll sure not stop there this time."

Well, Jack got 'way on past that house this time and got on down the road a piece and run up on all them boys comin' from the store.

"What'd ye get this time, Jack?"

Jack was so proud of this club he finally told 'em, and they begged him, said, "Oh, Jack! We got no wood in. If you'd just knock some in for us, we'll be awful much obliged."

So Jack went back with 'em and took out his club and told it to play away, and it went out on the hill, knocked down a big dead chestnut, knocked it right in the yard, and busted it every bit into firewood. All the boys just hollered when they saw that, said, "Just wait till father comes home now, Jack, and let him see what that club can do."

Well, they kept on after Jack to stay, till directly he said he'd wait a little while till their daddy came in. But Jack got very sleepy before that man came in and went off to sleep sittin' in his chair. And when the boys' father came home, Jack was a-sleepin' right on. They told him what kind of an outfit Jack had, and he says to 'em, says, "Hit's too dark now to knock up any more wood. Couldn't you boys try it out just a little on one of the big logs by the fireplace there?"

So the boys slipped the club out of Jack's hand real easy-like, and told it —

"Playaway, club! Playaway!
Break one log there on the pile."

The club started in on that log, banged away so loud it woke Jack up. Jack saw what was goin' on and jumped up and run out the door and hollered back,

"Playaway, club! Playaway!
Knock down the whole house!
Kill ever'body in it if they
don't hand here my tablecloth
and rooster, quick!"

And 'fore they knew it that club had knocked out every log on one side of the house and had started in on the roof. The boys came a-runnin' with Jack's tablecloth and rooster, says, "Jack! Jack! Stop that club quick and not let it kill us!"

Jack got his club and picked up his tablecloth and rooster and pulled out for home right then, even if it was after night.

About daylight Jack landed in home, and when he got in the house, his mother says to him, says, "Jack, that Wind's a-blowin' right on."

Jack says, "Never you mind about that. We got all we'll ever need now. This here's the right tablecloth and it'll furnish us all we want to eat. And this here rooster'll give us all the gold we'd ever want to spend,

so now we can buy some boards and nails and a new hammer handle and fix up the house against the North West Wind. And this here club'll keep in wood for us, all we want."

Jack's mother says to him, says, "I must see all that, Jack, before I know it's so."

So Jack took out his tablecloth and said,

"Spread, tablecloth! Spread!"

And he got his mother sat down and eat till they nearly busted. Then he got his rooster, says,

"Come, gold! Come!"

And there was his hat plumb full of gold eggs. Then he held out his club, says,

"Playaway, club! Playaway!"

And the club went out on the hill back of the house just a-bangin' and a-knockin' till it had a big pile of firewood all broke up in no time.

Jack's mother watched it and nearly died laughin' at it. She says to him, says, "Well Jack, you made out pretty well. We'll sure not be bothered about the North West Wind any more."

So Jack never did have to try to start out again to stop the cold Wind from blowin' in their house.

And he and his mother were both doin' pretty well, last time I saw 'em. They had that old rickety house fixed up tight against the Wind, too.

BEING NEIGHBORLY

The March family is one of the best known in American children's books. The four girls — Meg, Jo, Beth and Amy — work hard to help their mother manage while their father is away serving as a chaplain in the Civil War. Although they have many good times together, they sometimes worry about the Laurence boy next door, who lives in a splendid mansion but has only his stern grandfather for company.

"WHAT in the world are you going to do now, Jo?" asked Meg, one snowy afternoon, as her sister came tramping through the hall, in rubber boots, old sack and hood, with a broom in one hand and a shovel in the other.

"Going out for exercise," answered Jo, with a mischievous twinkle in her eyes.

"I should think two long walks this morning would have been enough! It's cold and dull out; and I advise you to stay warm and dry, by the fire, as I do," said Meg, with a shiver.

"Never take advice! Can't keep still all day, and, not being a pussy-cat, I don't like to doze by the fire. I like adventures, and I'm going to find some."

Meg went back to toast her feet and read *Ivanhoe*; and Jo began to dig paths with great energy. The snow was light, and with her broom she soon swept a path all round the garden, for Beth to walk in when the sun came out; and the invalid dolls needed air. Now the garden separated the Marches' house from that of Mr. Laurence. Both stood in a suburb of the city, which was still country-like, with groves and lawns, large gardens, and quiet streets. A low hedge parted the two estates. On one side was an old, brown house, looking rather bare and shabby,

robbed of the vines that in summer covered its walls, and the flowers which then surrounded it. On the other side was a stately stone mansion, plainly betokening every sort of comfort and luxury, from the big coach-house and well-kept grounds to the conservatory and the glimpses of lovely things one caught between the rich curtains. Yet it seemed a lonely, lifeless sort of house: for no children frolicked on the lawn, no motherly face ever smiled at the windows, and few people went in and out, except the old gentleman and his grandson.

To Jo's lively fancy, this fine house seemed a kind of enchanted palace, full of splendors and delights, which no one enjoyed. She had long wanted to behold these hidden glories, and to know the "Laurence boy," who looked as if he would like to be known, if he only knew how to begin. Since the party, she had been more eager than ever, and had planned many ways of making friends with him; but he had not been seen lately, and Jo began to think he had gone away, when she one day spied a brown face at an upper window, looking wistfully down into their garden, where Beth and Amy were snow-balling one another.

"That boy is suffering for society and fun," she said to herself. "His grandpa does not know what's good for him, and keeps him shut up all alone. He needs a party of jolly boys to play with, or somebody young and lively. I've a great mind to go over and tell the old gentleman so!"

The idea amused Jo, who liked to do daring things, and was always scandalizing Meg by her queer performances. The plan of "going over" was not forgotten; and when the snowy afternoon came, Jo resolved to try what could be done. She saw Mr. Laurence drive off, and then sallied out to dig her way down to the hedge, where she paused and took a survey. All quiet — curtains down at the lower windows; servants out of sight, and nothing human visible but a curly black head leaning on a thin hand at the upper window.

"There he is," thought Jo, "poor boy! all alone and sick this dismal day. It's a shame! I'll toss up a snowball, and make him look out, and then say a kind word to him."

Up went a handful of soft snow, and the head turned at once, showing a face which lost its listless look in a minute, as the big eyes brightened and the mouth began to smile. Jo nodded and laughed, and flourished her broom as she called out:

"How do you do? Are you sick?"

Laurie opened the window, and croaked out as hoarsely as a raven:

"Better, thank you. I've had a bad cold, and been shut up a week."

"I'm sorry. What do you amuse yourself with?"

"Nothing; it's as dull as tombs up here."

"Don't you read?"

"Not much; they won't let me."

"Can't somebody read to you?"

"Grandpa does, sometimes; but my books don't interest him and I hate to ask Brooke all the time."

"Have someone come and see you, then."

"There isn't anyone I'd like to see. Boys make such a row, and my head is weak."

"Isn't there some nice girl who'd read and amuse you? Girls are quiet, and like to play nurse."

"Don't know any."

"You know us," began Jo, then laughed, and stopped.

"So I do! Will you come, please?" cried Laurie.

"I'm not quiet and nice; but I'll come, if Mother will let me. I'll go ask her. Shut that window, like a good boy, and wait till I come."

With that, Jo shouldered her broom and marched into the house, wondering what they would all say to her. Laurie was in a flutter of excitement at the idea of having company, and flew about to get ready; for, as Mrs. March said, he was "a little gentleman," and did honor to the coming guest by brushing his curly pate, putting on a fresh collar, and trying to tidy up the room, which, in spite of half a dozen servants, was anything but neat. Presently there came a loud ring, then a decided voice, asking for "Mr. Laurie," and a surprised-looking servant came running up to announce a young lady.

"All right, show her up, it's Miss Jo," said Laurie, going to the door of his little parlor to meet Jo, who appeared, looking rosy and kind and quite at her ease, with a covered dish in one hand and Beth's three kittens in the other.

"Here I am, bag and baggage," she said briskly. "Mother sent her love, and was glad if I could do anything for you. Meg wanted me to bring some of her blancmange; she makes it very nicely, and Beth thought her cats would be comforting. I knew you'd laugh at them, but I couldn't refuse, she was so anxious to do something."

It so happened that Beth's funny loan was just the thing; for, in laughing over the kits, Laurie forgot his bashfulness, and grew sociable at once.

"That looks too pretty to eat," he said, smiling with pleasure, as Jo uncovered the dish, and showed the blancmange, surrounded by a garland of green leaves, and the scarlet flowers of Amy's pet geranium.

"It isn't anything, only they all felt kindly, and wanted to show it. Tell the girl to put it away for your tea; it's so simple, you can eat it; and, being soft it will slip down without hurting your sore throat. What a cozy room this is!"

"It might be if it was kept nice; but the maids are lazy, and I don't know how to make them mind. It worries me, though."

"I'll right it up in two minutes; for it only needs to have the hearth brushed, so — and the things made straight on the mantelpiece, so — and the books put here and the bottles there, and your sofa turned from the light, and the pillows plumped up a bit. Now, then, you're fixed."

And so he was; for, as she laughed and talked, Jo had whisked things into place, and given quite a different air to the room. Laurie watched her in respectful silence; and when she beckoned him to his sofa, he sat down with a sigh of satisfaction, saying gratefully:

"How kind you are! Yes, that's what it wanted. Now please take the big chair, and let me do something to amuse my company."

"No. I came to amuse you. Shall I read aloud?" and Jo looked affectionately toward some inviting books near by.

"Thank you; I've read all those, and if you don't mind I'd rather talk," answered Laurie.

"Not a bit; I'll talk all day if you'll only set me going. Beth says I never know when to stop."

"Is Beth the rosy one, who stays at home a good deal, and sometimes goes out with a little basket?" asked Laurie, with interest.

"Yes, that's Beth; she's my girl, and a regular good one she is, too."

"The pretty one is Meg, and the curly-haired one is Amy, I believe?"

"How did you find that out?"

Laurie colored up, but answered frankly, "Why, you see, I often hear you calling to one another, and when I'm alone up here, I can't help looking over at your house, you always seem to be having such good times. I beg your pardon for being so rude, but sometimes you forget to put down the curtain at the window where the flowers are; and when the lamps are lighted, it's like looking at a picture to see the fire, and you all round the table with your mother; her face is right opposite, and it looks so sweet behind the flowers, I can't help watching it. I haven't got any mother, you know," and Laurie poked the fire to hide a little twitching of the lips that he could not control.

The solitary, hungry look in his eyes went straight to Jo's warm

heart. She had been so simply taught that there was no nonsense in her head, and at fifteen she was as innocent and frank as any child. Laurie was sick and lonely; and, feeling how rich she was in home-love and happiness, she gladly tried to share it with him. Her face was very friendly and her sharp voice unusually gentle as she said:

"We'll never draw that curtain any more, and I give you leave to look as much as you like. I just wish, though, instead of peeping, you'd come over and see us. Mother is so splendid, she'd do you heaps of good, and Beth would sing to you if *I* begged her to, and Amy would dance; Meg and I would make you laugh over our funny stage properties, and we'd have jolly times. Wouldn't your grandpa let you?"

"I think he would, if your mother asked him. He's very kind, though he does not look so; and he lets me do what I like, pretty much, only he's afraid *I* might be a bother to strangers," began Laurie, brightening more and more.

"We are not strangers, we are neighbors, and you needn't think you'd be a bother. We want to know you, and I've been trying to do it this ever so long. We haven't been here a great while, you know, but we have got acquainted with all our neighbors but you."

"You see grandpa lives among his books, and doesn't mind much what happens outside. Mr. Brooke, my tutor, doesn't stay here, you know, and I have no one to go about with me, so I just stop at home and get on as I can."

"That's bad. You ought to make an effort, and go visiting everywhere you are asked; then you'll have plenty of friends, and pleasant places to go to. Never mind being bashful; it won't last long if you keep going."

Laurie turned red again, but wasn't offended at being accused of bashfulness; for there was so much goodwill in Jo, it was impossible not to take her blunt speeches as kindly as they were meant.

"Do you like your school?" asked the boy, changing the subject, after a little pause, during which he stared at the fire, and Jo looked about her, well pleased.

"Don't go to school; I'm a business man — girl, I mean. I go to wait on my great-aunt, and a dear, cross old soul she is, too," answered Jo.

Laurie opened his mouth to ask another question; but remembering just in time that it wasn't manners to make too many inquiries into people's affairs, he shut it again, and looked uncomfortable. Jo liked his good breeding, and didn't mind having a laugh at Aunt March, so she gave him a lively description of the fidgety old lady, her fat poodle, the parrot that talked Spanish, and the library where she reveled. Laurie enjoyed that immensely; and when she told about the prim old gentleman who came once to woo Aunt March, and in the middle of a fine speech, how Polly had tweaked his wig off, to his great dismay, the boy lay back and laughed till the tears ran down his cheeks, and a maid popped her head in to see what was the matter.

"Oh! that does me no end of good. Tell on, please," he said, taking his face out of the sofa cushions, red and shining with merriment.

Much elated with her success, Jo did "tell on," all about their plays and plans, their hopes and fears for father, and the most interesting events of the little world in which the sisters lived. Then they got to talking about books; and to Jo's delight, she found that Laurie loved them as well as she did, and had read even more than herself.

"If you like them so much, come down and see ours. Grandpa is out, so you needn't be afraid," said Laurie, getting up.

"I'm not afraid of anything," returned Jo, with a toss of the head.

"I don't believe you are!" exclaimed the boy, looking at her with much admiration, though he privately thought she would have good reason to be a trifle afraid of the old gentleman, if she met him in some of his moods.

The atmosphere of the whole house being summer-like, Laurie led the way from room to room, letting Jo stop to examine whatever struck her fancy; and so at last they came to the library, where she clapped her hands, and pranced, as she always did when especially delighted. It was lined with books, and there were pictures and statues and distracting little cabinets full of coins and curiosities, and sleepy-hollow chairs and queer tables, and bronzes; and, best of all, a great open fireplace, with quaint tiles all around it.

"What richness!" sighed Jo, sinking into the depth of a velvet chair, and gazing about her with an air of intense satisfaction. "Theodore Laurence, you ought to be the happiest boy in the world," she added impressively.

"A fellow can't live on books," said Laurie, shaking his head, as he perched on a table opposite.

Before he could say more, a bell rang, and Jo flew up, exclaiming with alarm, "Mercy me! it's your grandpa!"

"Well, what if it is? You are not afraid of anything, you know," returned the boy, looking wicked.

"I think I am a little bit afraid of him, but I don't know why I should be. Marmee said I might come, and I don't think you're any the worse for it," said Jo, composing herself, though she kept her eyes on the door.

"I'm a great deal better for it, and ever so much obliged. I'm only afraid you are very tired talking to me; it was *so* pleasant, I couldn't bear to stop," said Laurie, gratefully.

"The doctor to see you, sir," and the maid beckoned as she spoke.

"Would you mind if I left you for a minute? I suppose I must see him," said Laurie.

"Don't mind me. I'm as happy as a cricket here," answered Jo.

Laurie went away, and his guest amused herself in her own way. She was standing before a fine portrait of the old gentleman, when the door opened again, and without turning, she said decidedly, "I'm sure now that I shouldn't be afraid of him, for he's got kind eyes, though his mouth is grim, and he looks as if he had a tremendous will of his own. He isn't as handsome as *my* grandfather, but I like him."

"Thank you, ma'am," said a gruff voice behind her; and there, to her great dismay, stood old Mr. Laurence.

Poor Jo blushed till she couldn't blush any redder, and her heart began to beat uncomfortably fast as she thought what she had said. For a minute a wild desire to run away possessed her; but that was cowardly, and the girls would laugh at her; so she resolved to stay, and get out of the scrape if she could. A second look showed her that the living eyes, under the bushy gray eyebrows, were kinder even than the painted ones; and there was a sly twinkle in them which lessened her fear a good deal. The gruff voice was gruffer than ever, as the old gentleman said abruptly, after that dreadful pause, "So you're not afraid of me, hey?"

"Not much, sir."

"And you don't think me as handsome as your grandfather?"

"Not quite, sir."

"And I've got a tremendous will, have I?"

"I only said I thought so."

"But you like me, in spite of it?"

"Yes, I do, sir."

That answer pleased the old gentleman, he gave a short laugh, shook hands with her, and, putting his fingers under her chin, turned up her face, examined it gravely, and let it go, saying, with a nod, "You've got your grandfather's spirit, if you haven't his face. He *was* a fine man, my dear; but, what is better, he was a brave and honest one, and I was proud to be his friend."

"Thank you, sir"; and Jo was quite comfortable after that, for it suited her exactly.

"What have you been doing to this boy of mine, hey?" was the next question, sharply put.

"Only trying to be neighborly, sir"; and Jo told how her visit came about.

"You think he needs cheering up a bit, do you?"

"Yes, sir; he seems a little lonely, and young folks would do him good, perhaps. We are only girls, but we should be glad to help if we could, for we don't forget the splendid Christmas present you sent us," said Jo, eagerly.

"Tut, tut, tut! that was the boy's affair. How is the poor woman?"

"Doing nicely, sir"; and off went Jo, talking very fast, as she told all about the Hummels, in whom her mother had interested richer friends than they were.

"Just her father's way of doing good. I shall come and see your mother some fine day. Tell her so. There's the tea-bell; we have it early, on the boy's account. Come down, and go on being neighborly."

"If you'd like to have me, sir."

"Shouldn't ask you if I didn't"; and Mr. Laurence offered her his arm with old-fashioned courtesy.

"What _would_ Meg say to this?" thought Jo, as she was marched away, while her eyes danced with fun as she imagined herself telling the story at home.

"Hey! Why, what the dickens has come to the fellow?" said the old gentleman, as Laurie came running downstairs, and brought up with a start of surprise at the astonishing sight of Jo arm-in-arm with his redoubtable grandfather.

"I didn't know you'd come, sir," he began, as Jo gave him a triumphant little glance.

"That's evident, by the way you racket downstairs. Come to your tea, sir, and behave like a gentleman"; and having pulled the boy's hair

by way of a caress, Mr. Laurence walked on, while Laurie went through a series of comic evolutions behind their backs, which nearly produced an explosion of laughter from Jo.

The old gentleman did not say much as he drank his four cups of tea, but he watched the young people, who soon chatted away like old friends, and the change in his grandson did not escape him. There was color, light, and life in the boy's face now, vivacity in his manner, and genuine merriment in his laugh.

"She's right; the lad *is* lonely. I'll see what these little girls can do for him," thought Mr. Laurence, as he looked and listened. He liked Jo, for her odd, blunt ways suited him; and she seemed to understand the boy almost as well as if she had been one herself.

If the Laurences had been what Jo called "prim and poky" she would not have got on at all, for such people always made her shy and awkward; but finding them free and easy, she was so herself, and made a good impression. When they rose, she proposed to go, but Laurie said he had something more to show her, and took her away to the conservatory, which had been lighted for her benefit. It seemed quite fairlylike to Jo, as she went up and down the walks, enjoying the blooming walls on either side, the soft light, the damp, sweet air, and the wonderful vines and trees that hung above her — while her new friend cut the finest flowers till his hands were full; then he tied them up, saying, with the happy look Jo liked to see, "Please give these to your mother, and tell her I like the medicine she sent me very much."

They found Mr. Laurence standing before the fire in the great drawing room, but Jo's attention was entirely absorbed by a grand piano, which stood open.

"Do you play?" she asked, turning to Laurie with a respectful expression.

"Sometimes," he answered, modestly.

"Please do now. I want to hear it so I can tell Beth."

"Won't you first?"

"Don't know how; too stupid to learn, but I love music dearly."

So Laurie played, and Jo listened, with her nose luxuriously buried in heliotrope and tea-roses. Her respect and regard for the "Laurence boy" increased very much, for he played remarkably well, and didn't put on any airs. She wished Beth could hear him, but she did not say so; only praised him till he was quite abashed and his grandfather came to the rescue. "That will do, that will do, young lady. Too many sugar-plums are not good for him. His music isn't bad, but I hope he will do as well in more important things. Going? Well, I'm much obliged to you, and I hope you'll come again. My respects to your mother. Good night, Doctor Jo."

He shook hands kindly, but looked as if something did not please him. When they got into the hall, Jo asked Laurie if she had said anything amiss. He shook his head.

"No, it was me; he doesn't like to hear me play."

"Why not?"

"I'll tell you some day. John is going home with you, as I can't."

"No need of that; I am not a young lady, and it's only a step. Take care of yourself, won't you?"

"Yes; but you will come again, I hope?"

"If you promise to come and see us after you are well."

"I will."

"Good night, Laurie!"

"Good night, Jo, good night!"

When all the afternoon's adventures had been told, the family felt inclined to go visiting in a body, for each found something very attractive in the big house on the other side of the hedge; Mrs. March wanted to talk of her father with the old man who had not forgotten him; Meg longed to walk in the conservatory; Beth sighed for the grand piano; and Amy was eager to see the fine pictures and statues.

LOUISA MAY ALCOTT

"Mother, why didn't Mr. Laurence like to have Laurie play?" asked Jo, who was of an inquiring disposition.

"I am not sure, but I think it was because his son, Laurie's father, married an Italian lady, a musician, which displeased the old man, who is very proud. The lady was good and lovely and accomplished, but he did not like her, and never saw his son after he married. They both died when Laurie was a little child, and then his grandfather took him home. I fancy the boy, who was born in Italy, is not very strong, and the old man is afraid of losing him, which makes him so careful. Laurie comes naturally by his love of music for he is like his mother, and I dare say his grandfather fears that he may want to be a musician; at any rate, his skill reminds him of the woman he did not like, and so he 'glowered', as Jo said."

"Dear me, how romantic!" exclaimed Meg.

"How silly!" said Jo. "Let him be a musician, if he wants to, and not plague his life out sending him to college, when he hates to go."

"That's why he has such handsome black eyes and pretty manners, I suppose. Italians are always nice," said Meg, who was a little sentimental.

"What do you know about his eyes and his manners? You never spoke to him, hardly," cried Jo, who was *not* sentimental.

"I saw him at the party, and what you tell shows that he knows how to behave. That was a nice little speech about the medicine Mother sent him."

"He meant the blancmange, I suppose."

"How stupid you are, child! He meant you, of course."

"Did he?" and Jo opened her eyes as if it had never occurred to her before.

"I never saw such a girl! You don't know a compliment when you get it," said Meg, with the air of a young lady who knew all about the matter.

"I think they are great nonsense, and I'll thank you not to be silly, and spoil my fun. Laurie's a nice boy, and I like him, and I won't have any sentimental stuff about compliments and such rubbish. We'll all be good to him, because he hasn't got any mother, and he *may* come over and see us, mayn't he, Marmee?"

84

"Yes, Jo, your little friend is very welcome, and I hope Meg will remember that children should be children as long as they can."

"I don't call myself a child, and I'm not in my teens yet," observed Amy. "What do you say, Beth?"

"I was thinking about our *Pilgrim's Progress*," answered Beth, who had not heard a word. "How we got out of the Slough and through the Wicket Gate by resolving to be good, and up the steep hill by trying; and that maybe the house over there full of splendid things, is going to be our Palace Beautiful."

"We have got to get by the lions, first," said Jo, as if she rather liked the prospect.

MARK TWAIN

PIRATES

*A small town on the banks of the Mississippi River in the days of the
steamboats is just the place for a rascal like Tom Sawyer. He and his friends —
Joe Harper and Huckleberry Finn — are in and out of trouble regularly.
In this chapter from* The Adventures of Tom Sawyer, *both Tom and
Joe feel they have been mistreated and decide to run away.*

TOM'S mind was made up now. He was gloomy and desperate. He was a forsaken, friendless boy, he said; nobody loved him; when they found out what they had driven him to, perhaps they would be sorry; he had tried to do right and get along, but they would not let him; since nothing would do them but to be rid of him, let it be so; and let them blame him for the consequences — why shouldn't they? what right had the friendless to complain? Yes, they had forced him to it at last: he would lead a life of crime. There was no choice. By this time he was far down Meadow Land, and the bell for school to "take up" tinkled faintly upon his ear. He sobbed, now, to think he should never, never hear that old familiar sound any more — it was very hard, but it was forced on him; since he was driven out into the cold world, he must submit — but he forgave them. Then the sobs came thick and fast.

Just at this point he met his soul's sworn comrade, Joe Harper — hard-eyed, and with evidently a great and dismal purpose in his heart. Plainly here were "two souls with but a single thought." Tom, wiping his eyes with his sleeve, began to blubber out something about a resolution to escape from hard usage and lack of sympathy at home by roaming abroad into the great world, never to return; and ended by hoping that Joe would not forget him.

But it transpired that this was a request which Joe had just been going to make of Tom, and had come to hunt him up for that purpose. His mother had whipped him for drinking some cream which he had never tasted and knew nothing about; it was plain that she was tired of him and wished him to go; if she felt that way, there was nothing for him to do but to succumb; he hoped she would be happy, and never regret having driven her poor boy out into the unfeeling world to suffer and die.

As the two boys walked sorrowing along, they made a new compact to stand by each other and be brothers, and never separate till death relieved them of their troubles. Then they began to lay their plans. Joe was for being a hermit, and living on crusts in a remote cave, and dying, sometime, of cold, and want, and grief, but, after listening to Tom, he conceded that there were some conspicuous advantages about a life of crime, and so he consented to be a pirate.

Three miles below St. Petersburg, at a point where the Mississippi river was a trifle over a mile wide, there was a long, narrow, wooded island, with a shallow bar at the head of it, and this offered well as a rendezvous. It was not inhabited; it lay far over towards the farther shore, abreast a dense and almost wholly unpeopled forest. So Jackson's Island was chosen. Who were to be the subjects of their piracies was a matter that did not occur to them. Then they hunted up Huckleberry Finn, and he joined them promptly, for all careers were one to him; he was indifferent. They presently separated, to meet at a lonely spot on the river bank two miles above the village, at the favorite hour, which was midnight. There was a small log raft there which they meant to capture. Each would bring hooks and lines, and such provisions as he could steal in the most dark and mysterious way — as became outlaws; and before the afternoon was done, they had all managed to enjoy the sweet glory of spreading the fact that pretty soon the town would "hear something." All who got this vague hint were cautioned to "be mum and wait."

About midnight Tom arrived with a boiled ham and a few trifles, and stopped in a dense undergrowth on a small bluff overlooking the meeting-place. It was starlight, and very still. The mighty river lay like an ocean at rest. Tom listened a moment, but no sound disturbed the quiet. Then he gave a low, distinct whistle. It was answered from under the bluff. Tom whistled twice more; these signals were answered in the same way. Then a guarded voice said:

"Who goes there?"

"Tom Sawyer, the Black Avenger of the Spanish Main. Name your names."

"Huck Finn the Red-handed, and Joe Harper the Terror of the Seas." Tom had furnished these titles from his favorite literature.

"'Tis well. Give the countersign."

Two hoarse whispers delivered the same awful word simultaneously to the brooding night:

"BLOOD!"

Then Tom tumbled his ham over the bluff and let himself down after it, tearing both skin and clothes to some extent in the effort. There was an easy, comfortable path along the shore under the bluff, but it lacked the advantages of difficulty and danger so valued by a pirate.

The Terror of the Seas had brought a side of bacon, and had about worn himself out with getting it there. Finn the Red-handed had stolen a skillet, and a quantity of half-cured leaf-tobacco, and had also brought a few corn-cobs to make pipes with. But none of the pirates smoked or "chewed" but himself. The Black Avenger of the Spanish Main said it

would never do to start without some fire. That was a wise thought; matches were hardly known there in that day. They saw a fire smoldering upon a great raft a hundred yards above, and they went stealthily thither and helped themselves to a chunk. They made an imposing adventure of it, saying "hist" every now and then and suddenly halting with finger on lip; moving with hands on imaginary dagger-hilts; and giving orders in dismal whispers that if "the foe" stirred to "let him have it to the hilt," because "dead men tell no tales." They knew well enough that the raftmen were all down at the village laying in stores or having a spree, but still that was no excuse for their conducting this thing in an unpiratical way.

They shoved off presently, Tom in command, Huck at the left oar and Joe at the forward. Tom stood admidships, gloomy-browed and with folded arms, and gave his orders in a low, stern whisper.

"Luff, and bring her to the wind!"

"Aye, aye, sir!"

"Steady, stead-y-y-y!"

"Steady it is, sir!"

"Let her go off a point!"

"Point it is, sir!"

As the boys steadily and monotonously drove the raft toward midstream, it was no doubt understood that these orders were given only for "style," and were not intended to mean anything in particular.

"What sail's she carrying?"

"Courses, tops'ls, and flying-jib, sir!"

"Send the r'yals up! Layout aloft there, half a dozen of ye, foretomast-stuns'l! Lively, now!"

"Aye, aye, sir!"

"Shake out that mainto-galans'l! Sheets and braces! *Now*, my hearties!"

"Aye, aye, sir!"

"Hellum-a-lee — hard a-port! Stand by to meet her when she comes! Port, port! *Now*, men! With a will! Stead-y-y!"

"Steady it is, sir!"

The raft drew beyond the middle of the river; the boys pointed her head right and then lay on their oars. The river was not high, so there was not more than a two or three mile current. Hardly a word was said during the next three-quarters of an hour. Now the raft was passing before the distant town. Two or three glimmering lights showed where it lay, peacefully sleeping, beyond the vague vast sweep of star-gemmed water, unconscious of the tremendous event that was happening. The Black Avenger stood still with folded arms, "looking his last" upon the scene of his former joys and his later sufferings, and wishing "she" could see him, now abroad on the wild sea, facing peril and death with dauntless heart, going to his doom with a grim smile on his lips. It was but a small strain on his imagination to remove Jackson's Island beyond eye-shot of the village, and so he "looked his last" with a broken and satisfied heart. The other pirates were looking their last, too; and they all looked so long that they came near letting the current drift them out of the range of the island. But they discovered the danger in time, and made shift to avert it. About two o'clock in the morning the raft grounded on the bar two hundred yards above the head of the island, and they waded back and forth until they had landed their freight. Part of the little raft's belongings consisted of an old sail, and this they spread over a nook in the bushes for a tent to shelter their provisions; they themselves would sleep in the open air in good weather, as became outlaws.

They built a fire against the side of a great log twenty or thirty steps within the somber depths of the forest, and then cooked some bacon in the frying-pan for supper, and used up half of the corn "pone" stock they had brought. It seemed glorious sport to be feasting in that wild free way in the virgin forest of an unexplored and uninhabited island, far from the haunts of men, and they said they would never return to civilization. The climbing fire lit up their faces and threw its ruddy glare upon the pillared tree-trunks of their forest temple, and upon the varnished foliage and festooning vines. When the last crisp slice of bacon was gone, and the last allowance of corn pone devoured, the boys stretched themselves out on the grass, filled with contentment. They

could have found a cooler place, but they would not deny themselves such a romantic feature as the roasting campfire.

"*Ain't* it jolly?" said Joe.

"It's *nuts*," said Tom.

"What would the boys say if they could see us?"

"Say? Well, they'd just die to be here — hey, Hucky?"

"I reckon so," said Huckleberry; "anyways *I'm* suited. I don't want nothing better'n this. I don't ever get enough to eat gen'ally — and here they can't come and kick at a feller and bullyrag him so."

"It's just the life for me," said Tom. "You don't have to get up, mornings, and you don't have to go to school, and wash, and all that blame foolishness.

"You see a pirate don't have to do *anything*, Joe, when he's ashore, but a hermit *he* has to be praying considerable, and then he don't have any fun, any way, all by himself that way."

"Oh yes, that's so," said Joe, "but I hadn't thought much about it, you know. I'd a good deal ruther be a pirate now that I've tried it."

"You see," said Tom, "people don't go much on hermits, now-a-days, like they used to in old times, but a pirate's always respected. And a hermit's got to sleep on the hardest place he can find, and put sack-cloth and ashes on his head, and stand out in the rain, and —"

"What does he put sackcloth and ashes on his head for?" inquired Huck.

"*I* dunno. But they've *got* to do it. Hermits always do. You'd have to do that if you was a hermit."

"Dern'd if I would," said Huck.

"Well, what would you do?"

"I dunno. But I wouldn't do that."

"Why, Huck, you'd *have* to. How'd you get around it?"

"Why, I just wouldn't stand it. I'd run away."

"Run away? Well, you *would* be a nice old slouch of a hermit. You'd be a disgrace."

The Red-handed made no response, being better employed. He had finished gouging out a cob, and now he fitted a weed stem to it, loaded it with tobacco, and was pressing a coal to the charge and blowing a cloud of fragrant smoke; he was in the full bloom of luxurious contentment. The other pirates envied him this majestic vice, and secretly resolved to acquire it shortly. Presently Huck said:

"What do pirates have to do?"

Tom said:

"Oh, they have just a bully time — take ships, and burn them, and get the money and bury it in awful places in their island where there's ghosts and things to watch it, and kill everybody in the ships — make 'em walk a plank."

"And they carry the women to the island," said Joe; "they don't kill the women."

"No," assented Tom, "they don't kill the women — they're too noble. And the women's always beautiful, too."

"And don't they wear the bulliest clothes! Oh, no! All gold and silver and di'monds," said Joe with enthusiasm.

"Who?" said Huck.

"Why, the pirates."

Huck scanned his own clothing forlornly.

"I reckon I ain't dressed fitten for a pirate," said he, with a regretful pathos in his voice; "but I ain't got none but these."

But the other boys told him the fine clothes would come fast enough after they should have begun their adventures. They made him understand that his poor rags would do to begin with, though it was customary for wealthy pirates to start with a proper wardrobe.

Gradually their talk died out and drowsiness began to steal upon the eyelids of the little waifs. The pipe dropped from the fingers of the Red-handed, and he slept the sleep of the conscience-free and the weary. The Terror of the Seas and the Black Avenger of the Spanish Main had more difficulty in getting to sleep. They said their prayers inwardly, and lying down, since there was nobody there with authority to make them kneel and recite aloud; in truth they had a mind not to say them at all, but they were afraid to proceed to such lengths as that, lest they might call down a sudden and special thunder-bolt from heaven. Then at once they reached and hovered upon the imminent verge of sleep — but an intruder came now that would not "down." It was conscience. They began to feel a vague fear that they had been doing wrong to run away; and next they thought of the stolen meat, and then the real torture came. They tried to argue it away by reminding conscience that they had purloined sweetmeats and apples scores of times; but conscience was not to be appeased by such thin plausibilities. It seemed to them, in the end, that there was no getting around the stubborn fact that taking sweet-meats was only "hooking" while taking bacon and ham and such valu-ables was plain, simple stealing — and there was a command against that in the Bible. So they inwardly resolved that so long as they remained in the business, their piracies should not again be sullied with the crime of stealing. Then conscience granted a truce, and these curiously incon-sistent pirates fell peacefully to sleep.

H.W. LONGFELLOW

HIAWATHA'S CHILDHOOD

BY the shores of Gitche Gumee,
By the shining Big-Sea-Water,
Stood the wigwam of Nokomis,
Daughter of the Moon, Nokomis.
Dark behind it rose the forest,
Rose the black and gloomy pine-trees,
Rose the firs with cones upon them;
Bright before it beat the water,
Beat the clear and sunny water,
Beat the shining Big-Sea-Water.

There the wrinkled, old Nokomis
Nursed the little Hiawatha,
Rocked him in his linden cradle,
Bedded soft in moss and rushes,
Safely bound with reindeer sinews;
Stilled his fretful wail by saying,
"Hush! the Naked Bear will hear thee!"
Lulled him into slumber, singing,
"Ewa-yea! my little owlet!
Who is this, that lights the wigwam?
With his great eyes lights the wigwam?
Ewa-yea! my little owlet!"

Many things Nokomis taught him
Of the stars that shine in heaven;
Showed him Ishkoodah, the comet,
Ishkoodah, with fiery tresses;
Showed the Death-Dance of the spirits,
Warriors with their plumes and war-clubs,
Flaring far away to northward
In the frosty nights of Winter;
Showed the broad, white road in heaven,
Pathway of the ghosts, the shadows,
Running straight across the heavens,
Crowded with the ghosts, the shadows.

At the door on summer evenings
Sat the little Hiawatha,
Heard the whispering of the pine-trees,
Heard the lapping of the water,
Sounds of music, words of wonder;
"Minne-wawa!" said the pine-trees,
"Mudway-aushka!" said the water.

Saw the firefly, Wah-wah-taysee,
Flitting though the dusk of evening,
With the twinkle of its candle
Lighting up the brakes and bushes;
And he sang the song of children,
Sang the song Nokomis taught him:
"Wah-wah-taysee, little firefly
Little, flitting, white-fire insect,
Little, dancing, white-fire creature,
Light me with your little candle,
Ere upon my bed I lay me,
Ere in sleep I close my eyelids!"

Saw the moon rise from the water
Rippling, rounding from the water,
Saw the flecks and shadows on it,
Whispered: "What is that, Nokomis?"
And the good Nokomis answered:
"Once a warrior, very angry,
Seized his grandmother, and threw her
Up into the sky at midnight;
Right against the moon he threw her;
'Tis her body that you see there."

Saw the rainbow in the heaven,
In the eastern sky the rainbow,
Whispered: "What is that, Nokomis?"
And the good Nokomis answered:
" 'Tis the heaven of flowers you see there;
All the wild flowers of the forest,
All the lilies of the prairie,
When on earth they fade and perish,
Blossom in that heaven above us."

When he heard the owls at midnight,
Hooting, laughing in the forest,
"What is that?" he cried in terror;
"What is that," he said, "Nokomis?"
And the good Nokomis answered:
"That is but the owl and owlet,
Talking in their native language,
Talking, scolding at each other."

Then the little Hiawatha
Learned of every bird its language,
Learned their names and all their secrets,
How they built their nests in Summer,
Where they hid themselves in Winter,
Talked with them whene'er he met them,
Called them "Hiawatha's Chickens."

Of all beasts he learned the language,
Learned their names and all their secrets,
How the beavers built their lodges,
Where the squirrels hid their acorns,
How the reindeer ran so swiftly,
Why the rabbit was so timid,
Talked with them whene'er he met them,
Called them "Hiawatha's Brothers."

KATE DOUGLAS WIGGIN

ASHES OF ROSES

Rebecca Rowena Randall has left her loving but poor family and come to live with
her strong-minded Aunt Miranda and gentle Aunt Jane. The best part of
Rebecca's new life is the one-room school she attends. On this particular day, she is
looking forward to a very special afternoon program at the school.

ISS Dearborn dismissed the morning session at quarter to twelve, so that those who lived near enough could go home for a change of dress. Emma Jane and Rebecca ran nearly every step of the way, from sheer excitement, only stopping to breathe at the stiles.

"Will your aunt Mirandy let you wear your best or only your buff calico?" asked Emma Jane.

"I think I'll ask Aunt Jane," Rebecca replied. "Oh, if my pink was only finished! I left Aunt Jane making the buttonholes!"

"I'm going to ask my mother to let me wear her garnet ring," said Emma Jane. "It would look perfectly elegant flashing in the sun when I point to the flag. Good-bye; don't wait for me going back; I may get a ride."

Rebecca found the side door locked, but she knew that the key was under the step, and so, of course, did everybody else in Riverboro, for they all did about the same thing with it. She unlocked the door and went into the dining room to find her lunch laid on the table and a note from Aunt Jane saying that they had gone to Moderation with Mrs. Robinson in her carryall. Rebecca swallowed a piece of bread and butter and flew up the front stairs to her bedroom. On the bed lay the pink gingham dress finished by Aunt Jane's kind hands. Could she, dare she,

wear it without asking? Did the occasion justify a new costume, or would her aunts think she ought to keep it for the concert?

I'll wear it, thought Rebecca. *They're not here to ask, and maybe they wouldn't mind a bit; it's only gingham after all and wouldn't be so grand if it wasn't new, and hadn't tape trimming on it, and wasn't pink.*

She unbraided her two pigtails, combed out the waves of her hair and tied them back with a ribbon, changed her shoes, and then slipped on the pretty frock, managing to fasten all but the three middle buttons, which she reserved for Emma Jane.

Then her eyes fell on her cherished pink sunshade, the exact match, and the girls had never seen it. It wasn't quite appropriate for school, but she needn't take it into the room; she would wrap it in a piece of paper, just show it, and carry it coming home. She glanced in the parlor looking glass downstairs and was electrified at the vision. It seemed almost as if beauty of apparel could go no further than that heavenly pink gingham dress! The sparkle of her eyes, glow of her cheeks, sheen of her falling hair, passed unnoticed in the all-conquering charm of the rose-colored garment. Goodness! It was twenty minutes to one, and she would be late. She danced out the side door, pulled a pink rose from a bush at the gate, and covered the mile between the brick house and the seat of learning in an incredibly short time, meeting Emma Jane, also breathless and resplendent, at the entrance.

"Rebecca Randall!" exclaimed Emma Jane. "You're handsome as a picture!"

"I?" laughed Rebecca. "Nonsense! It's only the pink gingham."

"You're not good-looking every day," insisted Emma Jane, "but you're different somehow. See my garnet ring; Mother scrubbed it in soap and water. How on earth did your aunt Mirandy let you put on your bran'-new dress?"

"They were both away, and I didn't ask," Rebecca responded anxiously. "Why? Do you think they'd have said no?"

"Miss Mirandy always says no, doesn't she?" asked Emma Jane.

"Ye-es; but this afternoon is very special — almost like a Sunday school concert."

"Yes," assented Emma Jane, "it is, of course, with your name on the board, and our pointing to your flag, and our elegant dialogue, and all that."

The afternoon was one succession of solid triumphs for everybody concerned. There were no real failures at all, no tears, no parents ashamed of their offspring. Miss Dearborn heard many admiring remarks passed upon her ability and wondered whether they belonged to her or partly, at least, to Rebecca. The child had no more to do than several others, but she was somehow in the foreground. It transpired afterwards at various village entertainments that Rebecca couldn't be kept in the background; it positively refused to hold her. Her worst enemy could not have called her pushing. She was ready and willing and never shy, but she sought for no chances of display and was, indeed, remarkably lacking in self-consciousness, as well as eager to bring others into whatever fun or entertainment there was. If wherever the MacGregor sat was the head of the table, so in the same way wherever Rebecca stood was the center of the stage. Her clear, high treble soared above all the rest in the choruses, and somehow everybody watched her, took note of her gestures, her whole-souled singing, her irrepressible enthusiasm.

Finally it was all over, and it seemed to Rebecca as if she should never be cool and calm again, as she loitered on the homeward path. There would be no lessons to learn tonight, and the vision of helping with the preserves on the morrow had no terrors for her — fears could not draw breath in the radiance that flooded her soul. There were thick gathering clouds in the sky, but she took no note of them save to be glad that she could raise her sunshade. She did not tread the solid ground at all, or have any sense of belonging to the common human family, until she entered the side yard of the brick house and saw her aunt Miranda standing in the open doorway. Then with a rush she came back to earth.

"There she is, over an hour late; a little more, an' she'da been caught in a thundershower, but she'd never look ahead," said Miranda to Jane, "and added to all her other iniquities, if she ain't rigged out in that new dress, steppin' along with her father's dancin' school steps, and swingin' her parasol for all the world as if she was playactin'. Now I'm the oldest, Jane, an' I intend to have my say out; if you don't like it, you can go into the kitchen till it's over. Step right in here, Rebecca; I want to talk to you. What did you put on that good new dress for, on a school day, without permission?"

"I had intended to ask you at noontime, but you weren't at home, so I couldn't," began Rebecca.

"You did no such a thing; you put it on because you was left alone, though you knew well enough I wouldn't have let you."

"If I'd been *certain* you wouldn't have let me, I'd never have done it," said Rebecca, trying to be truthful, "but I wasn't *certain*, and it was worth risking. I thought perhaps you might, if you knew it was almost a real exhibition at school."

"Exhibition!" exclaimed Miranda scornfully. "You are exhibition enough by yourself, I should say. Was you exhibitin' your parasol?"

"The parasol *was* silly," confessed Rebecca, hanging her head, "but it's the only time in my whole life when I had anything to match it, and it looked so beautiful with the pink dress! Emma Jane and I spoke a dialogue about a city girl and a country girl, and it came to me just the minute before I started how nice it would come in for the city girl, and it did. I haven't hurt my dress a mite, Aunt Mirandy."

"It's the craftiness and underhandedness of your actions that's the worst," said Miranda coldly. "And look at the other things you've done! It seems as if Satan possessed you! You went up the front stairs to your room, but you didn't hide your tracks, for you dropped your handkerchief on the way up. You left the screen out of your bedroom window for the flies to come in all over the house. You never cleared away your lunch nor set away a dish, *and you left the side door unlocked* from half past twelve to three o'clock, so 't anybody coulda come in and stolen what they liked!"

Rebecca sat down heavily in her chair as she heard the list of her transgressions. How could she have been so careless? The tears began to flow now as she attempted to explain sins that never could be explained or justified.

"Oh, I'm so sorry!" she faltered. "I was trimming the schoolroom, and got belated, and ran all the way home. It was hard getting into my dress alone, and I hadn't time to eat but a mouthful, and just at the last minute, when I honestly — *honestly* — would have thought about clearing away and locking up, I looked at the clock and knew I could hardly get back to school in time to form in the line, and I thought how dreadful it would be to go in late and get my first black mark on a Friday afternoon, with the minister's wife and the doctor's wife and the school committee all there!"

"Don't wail and carry on now; it's no good cryin' over split milk," answered Miranda. "An ounce of good behavior is worth a pound of repentance. Instead of tryin' to see how little trouble you can make in a house that ain't your own home, it seems as if you tried to see how much you could put us out. Take that rose out o' your dress, and let me see the spot it's made on your yoke an' the rusty holes where the wet pin went in. No, it ain't, but it's more by luck than forethought. I ain't got any patience with your flowers and frizzled-out hair and furbelows an' airs an' graces, for all the world like your Miss Nancy father."

Rebecca lifted her head in a flash. "Look here, Aunt Mirandy, I'll be as good as I know how to be. I'll mind quick when I'm spoken to and never leave the door unlocked again, but I won't have my father called names. He was a p-perfectly l-lovely father, that's what he was, and it's *mean* to call him Miss Nancy!"

"Don't you dare answer me back that imperdent way, Rebecca, tellin' me I'm mean, your father was a vain, foolish, shiftless man, an' you might as well hear it from me as anybody else; he spent your mother's money and left her with seven children to provide for."

"It's s-something to leave s-seven nice children," sobbed Rebecca.

"Not when other folks have to help feed, clothe, and educate 'em," responded Miranda. "Now you step upstairs, put on your nightgown, go to bed, and stay there till mornin'. You'll find a bowl o' crackers an' milk on your bureau, an' I don't want to hear a sound from you till breakfasttime. Jane, run an' take the dish towels off the line, and shut the shed doors; we're goin' to have a turrible shower."

"We've had it, I should think," said Jane quietly as she went to do her sister's bidding. "I don't often speak my mind, Mirandy, but you ought not to have said what you did about Lorenzo. He was what he was and can't be made any different, but he was Rebecca's father, and Aurelia always says he was a good husband."

Miranda had never heard the proverbial phrase about the only "good Indian," but her mind worked in the conventional manner when she said grimly, "Yes, I've noticed that dead husbands are usually good ones; but the truth needs an airin' now and then, and that child will never amount to a hill o' beans till she gets some of her father trounced out of her. I'm glad I said just what I did."

"I daresay you are," remarked Jane, with what might be described as one of her annual bursts of courage, "but all the same, Miranda, it wasn't good manners, and it wasn't good religion!"

The clap of thunder that shook the house just at that moment made no such peal in Miranda Sawyer's ears as Jane's remark made when it fell with a deafening roar on her conscience.

Perhaps, after all, it is just as well to speak only once a year and then speak to the purpose.

Rebecca mounted the back stairs wearily, closed the door of her bedroom, and took off the beloved pink gingham with trembling fingers. Her cotton handerchief was rolled into a hard ball, and in the intervals of reaching the more difficult buttons that lay between her shoulder blades and her belt, she dabbed her wet eyes carefully, so that they should not rain salt water on the finery that had been worn at such a price. She smoothed it out carefully, pinched up the white ruffle at the neck, and laid it away in a drawer with an extra little sob at the toughness of life. The withered pink rose fell on the floor. Rebecca looked at it and thought, *Just like my happy day!* Nothing could show more clearly the kind of child she was than the fact that she instantly perceived the symbolism of the rose and laid it in the drawer with the dress as if she were burying the whole episode with all its sad memories. It was a child's poetic instinct with a dawning hint of woman's sentiment in it.

She braided her hair in the two accustomed pigtails, took off her best shoes (which had happily escaped notice), with all the while a fixed resolve growing in her mind, that of leaving the brick house and going back to the farm. She would not be received there with open arms — there was no hope of that — but she would help her mother about the house and send Hannah to Riverboro in her place. *I hope she'll like it!* she thought in a momentary burst of vindictiveness. She sat by the window trying to make some sort of plan, watching the lightning play over the hilltop and the streams of rain chasing each other down the lightning rod. And this was the day that had dawned so joyfully! It had been a red sunrise, and she leaned on the windowsill, studying her lesson and thinking what a lovely world it was. And what a golden morning! The changing of the bare, ugly little schoolroom into a bower of beauty; Miss Dearborn's pleasure at her success with the Simpson twins' recitation; the privilege of decorating the blackboard; the happy thought of drawing Columbia from the cigar box; the intoxicating moment when

the school clapped her! And what an afternoon! How it went on from glory to glory, beginning with Emma Jane's telling her, Rebecca Randall, that she was as "handsome as a picture."

She lived through the exercises again in memory, especially her dialogue with Emma Jane and her inspiration of using the bough-covered stove as a mossy bank where the country girl could sit and watch her flocks. This gave Emma Jane a feeling of such ease that she never recited better, and how generous it was of her to lend the garnet ring to the city girl, fancying truly how it would flash as she furled her parasol and approached the awestricken shepherdess! She had thought Aunt Miranda might be pleased that the niece invited down from the farm had succeeded so well at school, but no, there was no hope of pleasing her in that or in any other way. She would go to Maplewood on the stage next day with Mr. Cobb and get home somehow from Cousin Ann's. On second thoughts her aunts might not allow it. Very well, she would slip away now and see if she could stay all night with the Cobbs and be off next morning before breakfast.

Rebecca never stopped long to think, more's the pity, so she put on her oldest dress and hat and jacket, then wrapped her nightdress, comb, and toothbrush in a bundle and dropped it softly out of the window. Her room was in the L, and her window at no very dangerous distance from the ground, though had it been, nothing could have stopped her at that moment. Somebody who had gone on the roof to clean out the gutters had left a cleat nailed to the side of the house about halfway between the window and the top of the back porch. Rebecca heard the sound of the sewing machine in the dining room and the chopping of meat in the kitchen, so knowing the whereabouts of both her aunts, she scrambled out of the window, caught hold of the lightning rod, slid down to the helpful cleat, jumped to the porch, used the woodbine trellis for a ladder, and was flying up the road in the storm before she had time to arrange any details of her future movements.

Jeremiah Cobb sat at his lonely supper at the table by the kitchen window. "Mother," as he with his old-fashioned habits was in the habit of calling his wife, was nursing a sick neighbor. Mrs. Cobb was mother

only to a little headstone in the churchyard, where reposed "Sarah Ann, beloved daughter of Jeremiah and Sarah Cobb, aged seventeen months," but the name of Mother was better than nothing and served at any rate as a reminder of her woman's crown of blessedness.

The rain still fell, and the heavens were dark, though it was scarcely five o'clock. Looking up from his "dish of tea," the old man saw at the open door a very figure of woe. Rebecca's face was so swollen with tears and so sharp with misery that for a moment he scarcely recognized her. Then, when he heard her voice asking, "Please may I come in, Mr. Cobb?" he cried, "Well, I vow! It's my little lady passenger! Come to call on old Uncle Jerry and pass the time o' day, hev ye? Why, you're wet as sops. Draw up to the stove. I made a fire, hot as it was, thinkin' I wanted somethin' warm for my supper, bein' kind o' lonesome without Mother. She's settin' up with Seth Strout tonight. There, we'll hang your soppy hat on the nail, put your jacket over the chair rail, an' then you turn your back to the stove an' dry yourself good."

Uncle Jerry had never before said so many words at a time, but he had caught sight of the child's red eyes and tear-stained cheeks, and his big heart went out to her in her trouble, quite regardless of any circumstances that might have caused it.

Rebecca stood still for a moment until Uncle Jerry took his seat again at the table and then, unable to contain herself longer, cried, "Oh, Mr. Cobb, I've run away from the brick house, and I want to go back to the farm. Will you keep me tonight and take me up to Maplewood in the stage? I haven't got any money for my fare, but I'll earn it somehow afterwards."

"Well, I guess we won't quarrel 'bout money, you and me," said the old man, "and we've never had our ride together, anyway, though we allers meant to go downriver, not up."

"I shall never see Milltown now!" sobbed Rebecca.

"Come over here side o' me an' tell me all about it," coaxed Uncle Jerry. "Jest set down on that there wooden cricket an' out with the whole story."

Rebecca leaned her aching head against Mr. Cobb's homespun knee and recounted the history of her trouble. Tragic as that history seemed to her passionate and undisciplined mind, she told it truthfully and without exaggeration.

Uncle Jerry coughed and stirred in his chair a good deal during Rebecca's recital, but he carefully concealed any undue feeling of sympathy, just muttering, "Poor little soul! We'll see what we can do for her!"

"You will take me to Maplewood, won't you, Mr. Cobb?" begged Rebecca piteously.

"Don't you fret a mite," he answered, with a crafty little notion at the back of his mind. "I'll see the lady passenger through somehow. Now take a bit o' somethin' to eat, child. Spread some o' that tomato preserve on your bread; draw up to the table. How'd you like to set in Mother's place an' pour me out another cup o' hot tea?"

Mr. Jeremiah Cobb's mental machinery was simple and did not move very smoothly save when propelled by his affection or sympathy. In the present case these were both employed to his advantage, and mourning his stupidity and praying for some flash of inspiration to light his path, he blundered along, trusting to Providence.

Rebecca, comforted by the old man's tone and timidly enjoying the dignity of sitting in Mrs. Cobb's seat and lifting the blue china teapot, smiled faintly, smoothed her hair, and dried her eyes.

"I suppose your mother'll be turrible glad to see you back again?" queried Mr. Cobb.

A tiny fear — just a baby thing — in the bottom of Rebecca's heart stirred and grew larger the moment it was touched with a question.

"She won't like it that I ran away, I s'pose, and she'll be sorry that I couldn't please Aunt Mirandy; but I'll make her understand, just as I did you."

"I s'pose she was thinkin' o' your schoolin', lettin' you come down here, but land, you can go to school in Temperance, I s'pose?"

"There's only two months' school now in Temperance, and the farm's too far from all the other schools."

"Oh, well, there's other things in the world beside edjercation," responded Uncle Jerry, attacking a piece of apple pie.

"Ye-es, though Mother thought that was going to be the making of me," returned Rebecca sadly, giving a dry little sob as she tried to drink her tea.

"It'll be nice for you to be all together again at the farm — such a house full o' children!" remarked the dear old deceiver, who longed for nothing so much as to cuddle and comfort the poor little creature.

"It's too full — that's the trouble. But I'll make Hannah come to Riverboro in my place."

"S'pose Mirandy 'n' Jane'll have her? I should be 'most afraid they wouldn't. They'll be kind o' mad at your goin' home, you know, and you can't hardly blame 'em."

This was quite a new thought — that the brick house might be closed to Hannah since she, Rebecca, had turned her back upon its cold hospitality.

"How is this school down here in Riverboro — pretty good?" inquired Uncle Jerry, whose brain was working with an altogether unaccustomed rapidity — so much so that it almost terrified him.

"Oh, it's a splendid school! And Miss Dearborn is a splendid teacher!"

"You like her, do you? Well, you'd better believe she returns the compliment. Mother was down to the store this afternoon buyin' liniment for Seth Strout, an' she met Miss Dearborn on the bridge. They got to talkin' 'bout school, for Mother has summer-boarded a lot o' the schoolmarms an' likes 'em. 'How does the little Temperance girl git along?' asks Mother. 'Oh, she's the best scholar I have!' says Miss Dearborn. 'I could teach school from sunup to sundown if scholars was all like Rebecca Randall,' says she."

"Oh, Mr. Cobb, *did* she say that?" glowed Rebecca, her face sparkling and dimpling in an instant. "I've tried hard all the time, but I'll study the covers right off of the books now."

"You mean you would if you'd ben goin' to stay here," interposed Uncle Jerry. "Now ain't it too bad you've jest got to give it all up on account o' your aunt Mirandy? Well, I can't hardly blame ye. She's cranky an' she's sour; I should think she'd ben nussed on a bonnyclabber an' green apples. She needs bearin' with, an' I guess you ain't much on patience, be ye?"

"Not very much," replied Rebecca dolefully.

"If I'd had this talk with ye yesterday," pursued Mr. Cobb, "I believe I'd have advised ye different. It's too late now, an' I don't feel to say you've ben all in the wrong; but if 'twas to do over again, I'd say, well, your aunt Mirandy gives you clothes and board and schoolin' and is goin' to send you to Wareham at a big expense. She's turrible hard to get along with an' kind o' heaves benefits at your head, same's she would bricks; but they're benefits jest the same, an' mebbe it's your job to kind o' pay for 'em in good behavior. Jane's a leetle bit more easy-goin' than Mirandy, ain't she, or is she jest as hard to please?"

"Oh, Aunt Jane and I get along splendidly," exclaimed Rebecca; "she's just as good and kind as she can be, and I like her better all the time. I think she kind of likes me, too; she smoothed my hair once. I'd let her scold me all day long, for she understands, but she can't stand up for me against Aunt Mirandy; she's about as afraid of her as I am."

"Jane'll be real sorry tomorrow to find you've gone away, I guess, but never mind, it can't be helped. If she has a kind of a dull time with Mirandy, on account o' her bein' so sharp, why, of course, she'd set great store by your comp'ny. Mother was talkin' with her after prayer meetin' the other night. 'You wouldn't know the brick house, Sarah,' says Jane. 'I'm keepin' a sewin' school, an' my scholar has made three dresses. Wat do you think o' that,' says she, 'for an old maid's child? I've taken a class in Sunday school,' says Jane, 'an' think o' renewin' my youth an' goin' to the picnic with Rebecca,' says she, an' Mother declares she never seen her look so young 'n happy."

There was a silence that could be felt in the little kitchen, a silence only broken by the ticking of the tall clock and the beating of Rebecca's heart, which, it seemed to her, almost drowned the voice of the clock. The rain ceased, a sudden rosy light filled the room, and through the window a rainbow arch could be seen spanning the heavens like a radiant bridge. Bridges took one across difficult places, thought Rebecca, and Uncle Jerry seemed to have built one over her troubles and given her strength to walk.

"The shower's over," said the old man, filling his pipe; "it's cleared the air, washed the face o' the airth nice an' clean, an' everything tomorrer will shine like a new pin — when you an' I are drivin' upriver."

Rebecca pushed her cup away, rose from the table, and put on her hat and jacket quietly. "I'm not going to drive upriver, Mr. Cobb," she said, "I'm going to stay here and — catch bricks, catch 'em without throwing 'em back, too. I don't know as Aunt Mirandy will take me in after I've run away. But I'm going back now while I have the courage. You wouldn't be so good as to go with me, would you, Mr. Cobb?"

"You'd better b'lieve your Uncle Jerry don't propose to leave till he gits this thing fixed up," cried the old man delightedly. "Now you've had all you can stan' tonight, poor little soul, without gettin' a fit o' sickness, an' Mirandy'll be sore an' cross an' in no condition for argyment, so my plan is jest this: to drive you over to the brick house in my top buggy; to have you set back in the corner, an' I git out an' go to the side door; an' when I git your aunt Mirandy 'n' aunt Jane out int' the shed to plan for a load o' wood I'm goin' to have hauled there this week, you'll slip out o' the buggy and go upstairs to bed. The front door won't be locked, will it?"

"Not this time of night," Rebecca answered, "not till Aunt Mirandy goes to bed, but oh, what if it should be?"

"Well, it won't, an' if 'tis, why we'll have to face it out, though in my opinion there's things that won't bear facin' out an' had better be settled comfortable an' quiet. You see you ain't run away yet, you've only come over here to consult me 'bout runnin' away, an' we've concluded it ain't wuth the trouble. The only real sin you've committed, as

I figger it out, was in comin' here by the winder when you'd ben sent to bed. That ain't so very black, an' you can tell your aunt Jane 'bout it come Sunday, when she's chock-full o' religion, an' she can advise you when you'd better tell your aunt Mirandy. I don't believe in deceivin' folks, but if you've hed hard thoughts, you ain't obleeged to own 'em up; take 'em to the Lord in prayer, as the hymn says, and then don't go on hevin' 'em. Now come on; I'm all hitched up to go over to the post office; don't forget your bundle; 'it's always a journey, Mother, when you carry a nightgown'; them's the first words your Uncle Jerry ever heard you say! He didn't think you'd be bringin' your nightgown over to his house. Step in an' curl up in the corner; we ain't goin' to let folks see little runaway gals, 'cause they're goin' back to begin all over ag'in!"

When Rebecca crept upstairs and, undressing in the dark, finally found herself in her bed that night, though she was aching and throbbing in every nerve, she felt a kind of peace stealing over her. She had been saved from foolishness and error, kept from troubling her poor mother, prevented from angering and mortifying her aunts.

Her heart was melted now, and she determined to win Aunt Miranda's approval by some desperate means and to try and forget the one thing that rankled worst, the scornful mention of her father, of whom she thought with the greatest admiration and whom she had not yet heard criticized, for such sorrows and disappointments as Aurelia Randall had suffered had never been communicated to her children.

It would have been some comfort to the bruised, unhappy little spirit to know that Miranda Sawyer was passing an uncomfortable night and that she tacitly regretted her harshness, partly because Jane had taken such a lofty and virtuous position in the matter. She could not endure Jane's disapproval, although she would never have confessed to such a weakness.

As Uncle Jerry drove homeward under the stars, well content with his attempts at keeping the peace, he thought wistfully of the touch of Rebecca's head on his knee and the rain of her tears on his hand; of the sweet reasonableness of her mind when she had the matter put rightly before her; of her quick decision when she had once seen the path of duty; of the touching hunger for love and understanding that were so characteristic in her. "Lord A'mighty!" he ejaculated under his breath. "Lord A'mighty! To hector and abuse a child like that one! 'Tain't *abuse* exactly, I know, or 'twouldn't be to some o' your elephant-hided young ones, but to that tender will-o'-the-wisp a hard word's like a lash. Mirandy Sawyer would be a heap better woman if she had a little grave-stun to remember, same's Mother 'n' I have."

"I never seen a child improve in her work as Rebecca has today," remarked Miranda Sawyer to Jane on Saturday evening. "That settin' down I gave her was probably just what she needed, and I daresay it'll last for a month."

"I'm glad you're pleased," returned Jane. "A cringing worm is what you want, not a bright, smiling child. Rebecca looks to me as if she'd been through the Seven Years' War. When she came downstairs this morning, it seemed to me she'd grown old in the night. If you follow my advice, which you seldom do, you'll let me take her and Emma Jane down beside the river tomorrow afternoon and bring Emma Jane home to a good Sunday supper. Then, if you'll let her go to Milltown with the Cobbs on Wednesday, that'll hearten her up a little and coax back her appetite. Wednesday's a holiday on account of Miss Dearborn's going home to her sister's wedding, and the Cobbs and Perkinses want to go down to the Agricultural Fair."

EMILY DICKINSON

THE WIND BEGUN TO ROCK THE GRASS

THE wind begun to rock the grass
With threatening tunes and low, —
He flung a menace at the earth,
A menace at the sky.

The leaves unhooked themselves from trees
And started all abroad;
The dust did scoop itself like hands
And throw away the road.

The wagons quickened on the streets,
The thunder hurried slow;
The lightning showed a yellow beak,
And then a livid claw.

The birds put up the bars to nests,
The cattle fled to barns;
There came one drop of giant rain,
And then, as if the hands

That held the dams had parted hold,
The waters wrecked the sky,
But overlooked my father's house,
Just quartering a tree.

ALL KINDS OF PEOPLE

RICHARD KENNEDY

THE CONTESTS AT COWLICK

I was writing a story about a bell in a church steeple that was broken and didn't ring. It happened long ago, in Europe somewhere, and barbarian raiders arrived to sack and pillage the town, and the bell *had* to ring to call for help, but could not ring loud enough. The story got stuck at this place, and would not move until I set it in the Wild West, dressed the barbarian chief in a ten-gallon hat and six guns, and sent the sheriff off fishing.

HOGBONE and his gang rode into the little town of Cowlick one dusty afternoon when the sheriff and his men had gone fishing.

"If you need us," the sheriff said as they left, "we'll just be a holler up the creek."

So when the townsfolk saw Hogbone and his gang coming they hollered for the sheriff and his men. First the mayor hollered. Then the baker. Then the barber. Then several others tried it, and the banker hollered loudest of all. But when the sheriff and his men did not come, the townsfolk ran off to hide.

The streets were empty, doors latched, and windows locked as Hogbone and his gang rode up the main street. Here and there an eyeball showed at a knothole or between boards, and shadows moved with cat slowness behind curtains.

Hogbone and his fifteen men pulled up their horses in front of the bank. For the looks of it, Cowlick might have been a ghost town.

"Hey!" Hogbone yelled out. "Where's all the chickens in this coop? Hah? — how about it? Where's your sissy sheriff and his girl-friends? Bring 'em out so we can shoot 'em for a while!"

The shadows froze on the curtains, and not an eyeball showed.

"Well, shucks! This ain't no fun," Hogbone complained. "Heck!

Well, go git the money, boys." Scratching and spitting, some of the men got down off their horses. "Heck!" Hogbone said again. "I was looking for a little trouble."

At this moment Wally crawled out from under a horse trough and stood before the Hogbone gang.

"If you want some trouble," said Wally, "I can give you some trouble."

Hogbone dropped a look on the boy and said, "Most trouble you'd give me is stickin' between my teeth when I chaw you up."

"Har, har, har!" laughed the gang.

"Shut up!" said Hogbone.

"I'm the fastest runner anywhere around here," said Wally. "I bet I can win a footrace with your five best men."

"Well, ain't that a pretty how-de-do? I just reckon we might use a little fun." And Hogbone called out, "Alligator, Blackwhip, Snakebite, Gouge-eye, Crumby — git down here and do a little leg-stretching."

The men got down off their horses and Wally drew a line in the dust.

"We'll race down to the end of the street, around the corner and into McGee's Livery Stable," said Wally, getting down on the line. The five men hitched up their pants and kicked their spurs off, sailed their hats out of the way and dropped their gun belts. They hunched down on the line with Wally.

"Ready?" Wally said.

"Ready," the men grunted.

Hogbone held up his forty-four. "On your marks — get set — " BLAM!

The runners jolted across the line. Wally ran last — all the way down the street, and he was the last one around the corner. Some townsfolk came out of hiding as the runners raced by.

When Wally got to McGee's Livery Stable all five men were inside, laughing at him as he jogged up to the door. Wally smiled and slammed the heavy door on them and bolted it shut. He walked slowly back to Hogbone and the remaining ten men of the gang. A few more townsfolk were standing timidly about on the dusty street.

"They beat me," said Wally. "They got a drink and sprawled out in the straw."

"Har, har!" laughed Hogbone.

"Har, har, har!" laughed his men.

"Shut up!" growled Hogbone.

"I got a bad start or I could have beat them," Wally said. "So that didn't count much. But I'll give you another try. Pick five men and I bet I can climb faster than any of them."

"You're a sassy little mouse," said Hogbone. "What you need is a good whupping, and I got the men to do it." And he called out, "Horseblanket, Saddlehorn, Cinch, Rakespur, Yankbit, git over here!"

The five men got over there, grinning as they dropped their gun belts, took off their spurs and tucked at their shirts. More townsfolk came out to watch.

"We'll need two long ladders set up against the side of the church," said Wally. Some big boys ran off and got two twenty-foot ladders and set them up. Everyone stood around as Wally called out the rules of the contest. "Now, you five men go up that ladder and I go up the other one, and I mean to beat you all to the top and sit on the roof of the church first."

"This ought to be good," said Hogbone. "We might even have a neck-breaking." And he raised his forty-four.

BLAM!

The climbers jumped at their ladders and clambered up.

All five men were up and across the roof and sitting on the ridge-pole of the church before Wally was even at the top of his ladder. He stopped climbing and looked down. More townsfolk had come out of hiding to watch the contests. Some were carrying guns.

"Darn!" said Wally, looking up to the men on the roof above him. "You guys sure are good climbers."

"You ain't bad yourself for a sprout," said Horseblanket.

Wally yelled down to Hogbone. "They beat me fair, but I got one other contest I know I can beat those last five men at."

"Come on down off there, ya little rooster, and I'll give you a last chance," Hogbone yelled back.

Wally turned to the men on the roof again. "I'll bet you guys could outclimb a mountain goat."

"Ain't bad yourself, for a kid," said Saddlehorn.

"You guys comfortable up there? Can you see pretty good?" Wally asked.

"Just fine," said Rakespur.

"Best seat in the house," said Yankbit.

"It's a cinch," said Cinch.

So Wally left them on the roof and climbed down. By now there was a good crowd of townsfolk standing around.

"I know I don't look so strong," said Wally to Hogbone.

"Ya look like my little bitty sister," said Hogbone.

"Maybe so," Wally said, "but I can lift my horse over there." He pointed to a small pinto tied to a rail.

"I gotta see that," said Hogbone, "even if he is a runt horse."

"Okay," Wally said, "then it's a contest. I bet you I can lift my horse and I bet your five men they can't lift those big pigs they're riding."

Hogbone got red in the face and yelled, "Bump, Stump, Crump, Dump, Lump — git over here with your big — with your horses!" The men gathered around with their horses and Wally brought his pinto over.

"Now if you never lifted a horse before I can tell you it's a bit tricky," said Wally. "You have to get right underneath and lift straight up. Trouble is, the horse wants to slide off your back. So what you have to do is tie him on real tight. Here, get underneath your horses and I'll show you how it's done. Some of you people give a hand here," he said to the townsfolk.

Wally took a lasso from Bump's horse and tied it around over the top of the saddle and around under Bump's belly, and he took several loops like that and knotted the rope tight.

"That's how it's done," said Wally. The other men were tied under their horses the same way, tight up so just their feet and the tips of their fingers touched the ground.

"You sure got some pretty funny ideas," said Hogbone, studying the men under their horses.

"Pretty funny," said Wally. Then he walked over to the church and pulled both ladders away, and they slammed to the ground.

"Hey!" Yankbit shouted from the roof. "How we gonna git down from here?"

Right about then Hogbone began to catch on. He looked down the street where his runners had disappeared, then to the men on the roof, and then to the men tied underneath their own horses. He took out his forty-four and pointed it right between Wally's eyes. The townsfolk began to catch on, too, and a couple of the men pointed their rifles at Hogbone.

Wally spoke: "Now five of your men are locked in McGee's Livery Stable, and five are stuck on the church roof, and five are tied underneath their horses, and it looks like you can't do much alone."

"I can blow your head off," snarled Hogbone.

"Won't do you any good," said Wally, looking toward the men with rifles. "My friends here won't like that. Besides, you can have your men back and all the money in the bank if you can holler louder than me."

"Har, har!" laughed Hogbone. "A hollering contest? You think I got to be boss of this gang for nothing?"

"Har, har, har!" laughed his men.

"Shut up!" shouted Hogbone. The men shut up.

"You holler first," said Wally.

Hogbone scratched his chin and looked around very carefully. Then he shrugged and stuck his gun away in his holster.

"Okay," he said, "give me some air-sucking room." He spread his arms out and everyone moved back. Then he took a great breath of air and let out a holler.

"WHOOOOOOOOOOOOOOOOOOOOOOOOOAAAA-AAAAAAAAA!"

"Pretty good," said Wally, "but I can holler louder. You've got to bring it way up from deep in the stomach."

"You think I don't know that?" said Hogbone. "Listen. YOWWWWWWWWWWWWWWWWWWWWWWWW-WWWWOOOOOOOOOOOOOOOOOOO!"

"Not bad," said Wally, "but I can do better. If you took off your gun belt you could get more wind."

"That's a fact," agreed Hogbone, and he dropped his gun belt aside.

"HAAAAAAAAAAAAAAAAAAAAAAAAAAAAAAAAA-AAAEEEEEEEEEEEEEEEEEEEEYYYYYYYYYYY!"

"Take off your hat and toss your head back more," Wally suggested.

On his sixth try, Hogbone's hollers were still improving. On his seventh try the sheriff and his men, who had been just a holler up the creek, rode up quietly behind Hogbone and took him by the arms. Hogbone was so winded from hollering that he didn't even put up a fight when the sheriff hauled him off. The rest of the gang were rounded up and clapped in jail with him.

As Wally passed the jail window Hogbone glared out at him.

"Pretty funny," Hogbone snarled.

"Har, har, har!" laughed his men.

"Shut up!" said Hogbone.

Then Wally got together his fishing gear and headed up the creek.

LUCRETIA P. HALE

THE PETERKINS ARE OBLIGED TO MOVE

The Peterkins live in a village outside Boston in the days when a moving van was a cart pulled by horses. Mr. and Mrs. Peterkin have three older children — Agamemnon, Elizabeth Eliza and Solomon John — and several younger ones who are always called "the little boys." They are a very pleasant family, but even the simplest tasks always go wrong for them. Often it takes their friend, the lady from Philadelphia, to rescue the family from total confusion.

AGAMEMNON had long felt it an impropriety to live in a house that was called a "semi-detached" house, when there was no other "semi" to it. It had always remained wholly detached, as the owner had never built the other half. Mrs. Peterkin felt this was not a sufficient reason for undertaking the terrible process of a move to another house, when they were fully satisfied with the one they were in.

But a more powerful reason forced them to go. The track of a new railroad had to be carried directly through the place, and a station was to be built on that very spot.

Mrs. Peterkin so much dreaded moving that she questioned whether they could not continue to live in the upper part of the house and give up the lower part to the station. They could then dine at the restaurant, and it would be very convenient about traveling, as there would be no danger of missing the train, if one were sure of the direction.

But when the track was actually laid by the side of the house, and the steam-engine of the construction train puffed and screamed under the dining-room windows, and the engineer calmly looked in to see what the family had for dinner, she felt, indeed, that they must move.

But where should they go? It was difficult to find a house that

128

satisfied the whole family. One was too far off and looked into a tan-pit; another was too much in the middle of the town, next door to a machine-shop. Elizabeth Eliza wanted a porch covered with vines, that should face the sunset; while Mr. Peterkin thought it would not be convenient to sit there looking toward the west in the late afternoon (which was his only leisure time), for the sun would shine in his face. The little boys wanted a house with a great many doors, so that they could go in and out often. But Mr. Peterkin did not like so much slamming, and felt there was more danger of burglars with so many doors. Agamemnon wanted an observatory, and Solomon John a shed for a workshop. If he could have carpenters' tools and a workbench he could build an observatory, if it were wanted.

But it was necessary to decide upon something, for they must leave their house directly. So they were obliged to take Mr. Finch's, at the Corners. It satisfied none of the family. The porch was a piazza, and was opposite a barn. There were three other doors, too many to please Mr. Peterkin, and not enough for the little boys. There was no observatory, and nothing to observe if there were one, as the house was too low, and some high trees shut out any view. Elizabeth Eliza had hoped for a view; but Mr. Peterkin consoled her by deciding it was more healthy to have to walk for a view, and Mrs. Peterkin agreed that they might get tired of the same every day.

And everybody was glad a selection was made, and the little boys carried their india-rubber boots the very first afternoon.

Elizabeth Eliza wanted to have some system in the moving, and spent the evening in drawing up a plan. It would be easy to arrange everything beforehand, so that there should not be the confusion that her mother dreaded, and the discomfort they had in their last move. Mrs. Peterkin shook her head; she did not think it possible to move with any comfort. Agamemnon said a great deal could be done with a list and a programme.

Elizabeth Eliza declared if all were well arranged a programme would make it perfectly easy. They were to have new parlor carpets, which could be put down in the new house the first thing. Then the parlor furniture could be moved in, and there would be two comfortable rooms, in which Mr. and Mrs. Peterkin could sit while the rest of the move went on. Then the old parlor carpets could be taken up for the new dining-room and the downstairs bedroom, and the family could meanwhile dine at the old house. Mr. Peterkin did not object to this, though the distance was considerable, as he felt exercise would be good for them all. Elizabeth Eliza's programme then arranged that the dining-room furniture should be moved the third day, by which time one of the old parlor carpets would be down in the new dining-room, and they could still sleep in the old house. Thus there would always be a quiet, comfortable place in one house or the other. Each night, when Mr. Peterkin came home, he would find some place for quiet thought and rest, and each day there should be moved only the furniture needed for a certain room. Great confusion would be avoided and nothing misplaced. Elizabeth Eliza wrote these last words at the head of her programme — "Misplace nothing." And Agamemnon made a copy of the programme for each member of the family.

The first thing to be done was to buy the parlor carpets. Elizabeth Eliza had already looked at some in Boston, and the next morning she went, by an early train, with her father, Agamemnon, and Solomon John, to decide upon them.

They got home about eleven o'clock, and when they reached the house were dismayed to find two furniture wagons in front of the gate, already partly filled! Mrs. Peterkin was walking in and out of the open door, a large book in one hand, and a duster in the other, and she came to meet them in an agony of anxiety. What should they do? The furniture carts had appeared soon after the rest had left for Boston, and the men insisted upon beginning to move the things. In vain had she shown Elizabeth Eliza's programme; in vain had she insisted they must take only the parlor furniture. They had declared they must put the heavy pieces in the bottom of the cart, and the lighter furniture on top. So she had seen them go into every room in the house, and select one piece of furniture after another, without even looking at Elizabeth Eliza's programme; she doubted if they could read it if they had looked at it.

Mr. Peterkin had ordered the carters to come; but he had no idea they would come so early, and supposed it would take them a long time to fill the carts.

But they had taken the dining-room sideboard first, — a heavy piece of furniture, — and all its contents were now on the dining-room table. Then, indeed, they selected the parlor bookcase, but had set every book on the floor. The men had told Mrs. Peterkin they would put the books in the bottom of the cart, very much in the order they were taken from the shelves. But by this time Mrs. Peterkin was considering the carters as natural enemies, and dared not trust them; besides, the books ought all to be dusted. So she was now holding one of the volumes of Agamemnon's Encyclopedia, with difficulty, in one hand, while she was dusting it with the other. Elizabeth Eliza was in dismay. At this moment four men were bringing down a large chest of drawers from her father's room, and they called to her to stand out of the way. The parlor was a scene of confusion. In dusting the books Mrs. Peterkin neglected to restore them to the careful rows in which they were left by the men, and they lay in hopeless masses in different parts of the room. Elizabeth Eliza sunk in despair upon the end of a sofa.

"It would have been better to buy the red and blue carpet," said Solomon John.

"Is not the carpet bought?" exclaimed Mrs. Peterkin. And then they were obliged to confess they had been unable to decide upon one, and had come back to consult Mrs. Peterkin.

"What shall we do?" asked Mrs. Peterkin.

Elizabeth Eliza rose from the sofa and went to the door, saying, "I shall be back in a moment."

Agamemnon slowly passed round the room, collecting the scattered volumes of his Encyclopedia. Mr. Peterkin offered a helping hand to a man lifting a wardrobe.

Elizabeth Eliza soon returned. "I did not like to go and ask her. But I felt that I must in such an emergency. I explained to her the whole matter, and she thinks we should take the carpet at Makillan's."

"Makillan's" was a store in the village, and the carpet was the only one all the family had liked without any doubt; but they had supposed they might prefer one from Boston.

The moment was a critical one. Solomon John was sent directly to Makillan's to order the carpet to be put down that very day. But where should they dine? where should they have their supper? and where was Mr. Peterkin's "quiet hour"? Elizabeth Eliza was frantic; the dining-room floor and table were covered with things.

It was decided that Mr. and Mrs. Peterkin should dine at the Bromwicks, who had been most neighborly in their offers, and the rest should get something to eat at the baker's.

Agamemnon and Elizabeth Eliza hastened away to be ready to receive the carts at the other house, and direct the furniture as they could. After all there was something exhilarating in this opening of the new house, and in deciding where things should go. Gaily Elizabeth Eliza stepped down the front garden of the new home and across the piazza, and to the door. But it was locked, and she had no keys!

"Agamemnon, did you bring the keys?" she exclaimed.

No, he had not seen them since the morning, — when — ah! — yes, the little boys were allowed to go to the house for their india-rubber boots, as there was a threatening of rain. Perhaps they had left some door unfastened — perhaps they had put the keys under the door-mat. No, each door, each window, was solidly closed, and there was no mat!

"I shall have to go to the school to see if they took the keys with them," said Agamemnon; "or else go home to see if they left them there." The school was in a different direction from the house, and far at the other end of the town; for Mr. Peterkin had not yet changed the boys' school, as he proposed to do after their move.

"That will be the only way," said Elizabeth Eliza, for it had been arranged that the little boys should take their lunch to school, and not come home at noon.

She sat down on the steps to wait, but only for a moment, for the carts soon appeared, turning the corner. What should be done with the furniture? Of course the carters must wait for the keys, as she should need them to set the furniture up in the right places. But they could not stop for this. They put it down upon the piazza, on the steps, in the garden, and Elizabeth Eliza saw how incongruous it was! There was something from every room in the house! Even the large family chest, which had proved too heavy for them to travel with, had come down from the attic, and stood against the front door.

And Solomon John appeared with the carpet-woman, and a boy with a wheelbarrow, bringing the new carpet. And all stood and waited. Some opposite neighbors appeared to offer advice and look on, and Elizabeth Eliza groaned inwardly that only the shabbiest of their furniture appeared to be standing full in view.

It seemed ages before Agamemnon returned, and no wonder; for he had been to the house, then to the school, then back to the house, for one of the little boys had left the keys at home, in the pocket of his clothes. Meanwhile the carpet-woman had waited, and the boy with the wheelbarrow had waited, and when they got in they found the parlor must be swept and cleaned. So the carpet-woman went off in dudgeon,

for she was sure there would not be time enough to do anything.

And one of the carts came again, and in their hurry the men set the furniture down anywhere. Elizabeth Eliza was hoping to make a little place in the dining-room, where they might have their supper, and go home to sleep. But she looked out, and there were the carters bringing the bedsteads, and proceeding to carry them upstairs.

In despair Elizabeth Eliza went back to the old house. If she had been there she might have prevented this. She found Mrs. Peterkin in an agony about the entry oil-cloth. It had been made in the house, and how could it be taken out of the house? Agamemnon made measurements; it certainly could not go out of the front door! He suggested it might be left till the house was pulled down, when it could easily be moved out of one side. But Elizabeth Eliza reminded him that the whole house was to be moved without being taken apart. Perhaps it could be cut in strips narrow enough to go out. One of the men loading the remaining cart disposed of the question by coming in and rolling up the oil-cloth and carrying it off on top of his wagon.

Elizabeth Eliza felt she must hurry back to the new house. But what should they do? — no beds here, no carpets there! The dining-room table and sideboard were at the other house, the plates, and forks, and spoons here. In vain she looked at her programme. It was all reversed; everything was misplaced. Mr. Peterkin would suppose they were to eat here and sleep here, and what had become of the little boys?

Meanwhile the man with the first cart had returned. They fell to packing the dining-room china.

They were up in the attic, they were down in the cellar. Every one suggested to take the tacks out of the parlor carpets, as they should want to take them next. Mrs. Peterkin sunk upon a kitchen chair.

"Oh, I wish we had decided to stay and be moved in the house!" she exclaimed.

Solomon John urged his mother to go to the new house, for Mr. Peterkin would be there for his "quiet hour." And when the carters at last appeared, carrying the parlor carpets on their shoulders, she sighed and said, "There is nothing left," and meekly consented to be led away.

They reached the new house to find Mr. Peterkin sitting calmly in a rocking chair on the piazza, watching the oxen coming into the opposite barn. He was waiting for the keys, which Solomon John had taken back with him. The little boys were in a horse-chestnut tree, at the side of the house.

Agamemnon opened the door. The passages were crowded with furniture, the floors were strewn with books; the bureau was upstairs that was to stand in a lower bedroom; there was not a place to lay a table, — there was nothing to lay upon it; for the knives and plates and spoons had not come, and although the tables were there they were covered with chairs and boxes.

At this moment came a covered basket from the lady from Philadelphia. It contained a choice supper, and forks and spoons, and at the same moment appeared a pot of hot tea from an opposite neighbor. They placed all this on the back of a bookcase lying upset, and sat around it. Solomon John came rushing in from the gate.

"The last load is coming! We are all moved!" he exclaimed; and the little boys joined in a chorus, "We are moved! we are moved!"

Mrs. Peterkin looked sadly round; the kitchen utensils were lying on the parlor lounge, and an old family gun on Elizabeth Eliza's hat-box. The parlor clock stood on a barrel; some coal-scuttles had been placed on the parlor table, a bust of Washington stood in the door-way, and the looking-glasses leaned against the pillars of the piazza. But they were moved! Mrs. Peterkin felt, indeed, that they were very much moved.

JAMES WHITCOMB RILEY
LITTLE ORPHANT ANNIE

ITTLE Orphant Annie's come to our house to stay,
An' wash the cups an' saucers up, an' brush the
  crumbs away,
An' shoo the chickens off the porch, an' dust the
  hearth, an' sweep,
An' make the fire, an' bake the bread, an' earn her
  board-an'-keep;
An' all us other children, when the supper-things
  is done,
We set around the kitchen fire an' has the mostest fun
A-list'nin' to the witch-tales 'at Annie tells about,
An' the Gobble-uns 'at gits you
          Ef you
                Don't
                    Watch
                        Out!

Wunst they wuz a little boy wouldn't say his prayers, —
An' when he went to bed at night, away up-stairs,
His Mammy heered him holler, an' his Daddy heered him bawl,
An' when they turn't the kivvers down, he wuzn't there at all!
An' they seeked him in the rafter-room, an' cubby-hole, an' press,

An' seeked him up the chimbly-flue, an' ever'-wheres, I guess;
But all they ever found wuz thist his pants an' roundabout: —
An' the Gobble-uns 'll git you
     Ef you
         Don't
             Watch
                 Out!

An' one time a little girl 'ud allus laugh an' grin,
An' make fun of ever' one, an' all her blood-an'-kin;
An' wunst, when they was "company," an' ole folks was there,
She mocked 'em an' shocked 'em, an' said she didn't care!
An' thist as she kicked her heels, an' turn't to run an' hide,
They was two great Black Things a-standin' by her side,
An' they snatched her through the ceilin' 'fore she knowed what she's
    about!
An' the Gobble-uns 'll git you
     Ef you
         Don't
             Watch
                 Out!

An' little Orphant Annie says, when the blaze is blue,
An' the lamp-wick sputters, an' the wind goes *woo-oo!*
An' you hear the crickets quit, an' the moon is gray,
An' the lightnin'-bugs in dew is all squenched away, —
You better mind yer parunts, an' yer teachers fond an' dear,
An' churish them 'at loves you, an' dry the orphant's tear,
An' he'p the pore an' needy ones 'at clusters all about,
Er the Gobble-uns 'll git you
     Ef you
         Don't
             Watch
                 Out!

KATHERINE PATERSON

HARASSING MISS HARRIS

Gilly Hopkins is eleven years old and has spent most of her life moving from one foster home to another. She trusts no one and has found many ways to confuse and antagonize anyone who tries to help her, including Mrs. Trotter, her new foster mother; William Ernest Teague, another foster child in the Trotter home; and Mr. Randolph, an elderly neighbor. In this story, she is faced with a new teacher who seems to ignore her tricks.

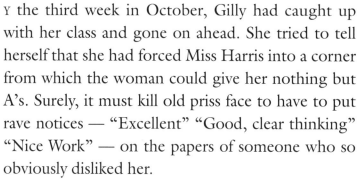

BY the third week in October, Gilly had caught up with her class and gone on ahead. She tried to tell herself that she had forced Miss Harris into a corner from which the woman could give her nothing but A's. Surely, it must kill old priss face to have to put rave notices — "Excellent" "Good, clear thinking" "Nice Work" — on the papers of someone who so obviously disliked her.

But Miss Harris was a cool customer. If she knew that Gilly despised her, she never let on. So at this point Gilly was not ready to pull her time-honored trick of stopping work just when the teacher had become convinced that she had a bloody genius on her hands. That had worked so beautifully at Hollywood Gardens — the whole staff had gone totally ape when suddenly one day she began turning in blank sheets of paper. It was the day after Gilly had overheard the principal telling her teacher that Gilly had made the highest score in the entire school's history on her national aptitude tests, but, of course, no one knew that she knew, so an army of school psychologists had been called in to try to figure her out. Since no one at school would take the blame for Gilly's sudden refusal to achieve, they decided to blame her foster parents, which made Mrs. Nevins so furious that she demanded that Miss Ellis remove Gilly at once instead of waiting out the year — the

year Mrs. Nevins had reluctantly agreed to, after her first complaints about Gilly's sassy and underhanded ways.

But something warned Gilly that Miss Harris was not likely to crumble at the sight of a blank sheet of paper. She was more likely simply to ignore it. She was different from the other teachers Gilly had known. She did not appear to be dependent on her students. There was no evidence that they fed either her anxieties or her satisfactions. In Gilly's social-studies book there was a picture of a Muslim woman of Saudi Arabia, with her body totally covered except for her eyes. It reminded Gilly somehow of Miss Harris, who had wrapped herself up in invisible robes. Once or twice a flash in the eyes seemed to reveal something to Gilly of the person underneath the protective garments, but such flashes were so rare that Gilly hesitated to say even to herself what they might mean.

Some days it didn't matter to Gilly what Miss Harris was thinking or not thinking. It was rather comfortable to go to school with no one yelling or cajoling — to know that your work was judged on its merits and was not affected by the teacher's personal opinion of the person doing the work. It was a little like throwing a basketball. If you aimed right, you got it through the hoop; it was absolutely just and absolutely impersonal.

But other days, Miss Harris's indifference grated on Gilly. She was not used to being treated like everyone else. Ever since the first grade, she had forced her teachers to make a special case of her. She had been in charge of her own education. She had learned what and when it pleased her. Teachers had courted her and cursed her, but no one before had simply melted her into the mass.

As long as she had been behind the mass, she tolerated this failure to treat her in a special manner, but now, even the good-morning smile seemed to echo the math computer's "Hello, Gilly number 58706, today we will continue our study of fractions." *Crossing threshold of classroom causes auto-teacher to light up and say "Good morning." For three thousand dollars additional, get the personalized electric-eye model that calls each student by name.*

For several days she concentrated on the vision of a computer-activated Miss Harris. It seemed to fit. Brilliant, cold, totally, absolutely, and maddeningly fair, all her inner workings shinily encased and hidden from view. Not a Muslim but a flawless tamperproof machine.

The more Gilly thought about it, the madder she got. No one had a right to cut herself off from other people like that. Just once, before she left this dump, she'd like to pull a wire inside that machine. Just once she'd like to see Harris-6 scream in anger — fall apart — break down.

But Miss Harris wasn't like Trotter. You didn't have to be around Trotter five minutes before you knew the direct route to her insides — William Ernest Teague. Miss Harris wasn't hooked up to other people. It was like old *Mission Impossible* reruns on TV: *Your mission, if you decide to accept it, is to get inside this computerized robot, discover how it operates, and neutralize its effectiveness.* The self-destructing tape never told the mission-impossible team how to complete their impossible mission, but the team always seemed to know. Gilly, on the other hand, hadn't a clue.

It was TV that gave her the clue. She hadn't been thinking about Miss Harris at all. She'd been thinking, actually, of how to get the rest of Mr. Randolph's money and hadn't been listening to the news broadcast. Then somehow it began sending a message into her brain. A high government official had told a joke on an airplane that had gotten him fired. Not just any joke, mind you. A dirty joke. But that wasn't what got him fired. The dirty joke had been somehow insulting to blacks. Apparently all the black people in the country and even some whites were jumping up and down with rage. Unfortunately the commentator didn't repeat the joke. She could have used it. But at least she knew now something that might be a key to Harris-6.

She borrowed some money from Trotter for "school supplies," and bought a pack of heavy white construction paper and magic markers. Behind the closed door of her bedroom she began to make a greeting card, fashioning it as closely as she could to the tall, thin, "comic" cards on the special whirlaround stand in the drugstore.

At first she tried to draw a picture on the front, wasting five or six

precious sheets of paper in the attempt. Cursing her incompetence, she stole one of Trotter's magazines and cut from it a picture of a tall, beautiful black woman in an Afro. Her skin was a little darker than Miss Harris's, but it was close enough.

Above the picture of the woman she lettered these words carefully (she could print well, even if her drawing stank):

They're saying "Black is beautiful!"

Then below the picture:

But the best that I can figger
Is everyone who's saying so
Looks mighty like a

And inside in tiny letters:

person with a vested interest in
maintaining this point of view.

She had to admit it. It was about the funniest card she'd ever seen in her life. Gifted Gilly — a funny female of the first rank. If her bedroom had been large enough, she'd have rolled on the floor. As it was, she lay on the bed hugging herself and laughing until she was practically hysterical. Her only regret was that the card was to be anonymous. She would have enjoyed taking credit for this masterpiece.

She got to school very early the next morning and sneaked up the smelly stairs to Harris-6 before the janitor had even turned on the hall lights. For a moment she feared that the door might be locked, but it opened easily under her hand. She slipped the card into the math book that lay in the middle of Miss Harris's otherwise absolutely neat desk. She wanted to be sure that no one else would discover it and ruin everything.

All day long, but especially during math, Gilly kept stealing glances

at Miss Harris. Surely at any minute, she would pick up the book. Surely she could see the end of the card sticking out and would be curious. But Miss Harris left the book exactly where it was. She borrowed a book from a student when she needed to refer to one. It was as though she sensed her own was booby-trapped.

By lunchtime Gilly's heart, which had started the day jumping with happy anticipation, was kicking angrily at her stomach. By midafternoon she was so mad that nothing had happened that she missed three spelling words, all of which she knew perfectly well. At the three o'clock bell, she slammed her chair upside down on her desk and headed for the door.

"Gilly."

Her heart skipped as she turned toward Miss Harris.

"Will you wait a minute, please?"

They both waited, staring quietly at each other until the room emptied. Then Miss Harris got up from her desk and closed the door. She took a chair from one of the front desks and put it down a little distance from her own. "Sit down for a minute, won't you?"

Gilly sat. The math book lay apparently undisturbed, the edge of the card peeping out at either end.

"You may find this hard to believe, Gilly, but you and I are very much alike."

Gilly snapped to attention despite herself.

"I don't mean in intelligence, although that is true, too. Both of us are smart, and we know it. But the thing that brings us closer than intelligence is anger. You and I are two of the angriest people I know." She said all this in a cool voice that cut each word in a thin slice from the next and then waited, as if to give Gilly a chance to challenge her. But Gilly was fascinated, like the guys in the movies watching the approach of a cobra. She wasn't about to make a false move.

"We do different things with our anger, of course. I was always taught to deny mine, which I did and still do. And that makes me envy you. Your anger is still up here on the surface where you can look it in the face, make friends with it if you want to."

She might have been talking Swahili for all Gilly could understand.

"But I didn't ask you to stay after school to tell you how intelligent you are or how much I envy you, but to thank you for your card."

It had to be sarcasm, but Harris-6 was smiling almost like a human being. When did the cobra strike?

"I took it to the teachers' room at noon and cursed creatively for twenty minutes. I haven't felt so good in years."

She'd gone mad like the computer in *2001*. Gilly got up and started backing toward the door. Miss Harris just smiled and made no effort to stop her. As soon as she got to the stairs, Gilly began to run and, cursing creatively, ran all the way home.

ELOISE GREENFIELD

WAY DOWN IN THE MUSIC

I GET way down in the music
Down inside the music
I let it wake me
      take me
Spin me around and make me
Uh-get down

Inside the sound of the Jackson Five
Into the tune of Earth, Wind and Fire
Down in the bass where the beat comes from
Down in the horn and down in the drum
    I get down
    I get down

    I get way down in the music
    Down inside the music
  I let it wake me
      take me
Spin me around and shake me
I get down, down
I get down

EDNA ST. VINCENT MILLAY

AFTERNOON ON
A HILL

I WILL be the gladdest thing
    Under the sun!
I will touch a hundred flowers
    And not pick one.

I will look at cliffs and clouds
    With quiet eyes,
Watch the wind bow down the grass,
    And the grass rise.

And when lights begin to show
    Up from the town,
I will mark which must be mine,
    And then start down!

BETSY BYARS

A PUPPY FOR HARVEY

Carlie, Thomas J and Harvey have all come to live in the same foster home.
Harvey is there because his father ran over him in his car and broke his legs.
He worries that it may not have been an accident, and his despair only increases
as the summer goes on. Now one leg is infected and he is in the hospital
with no interest, it appears, in getting well. However, Carlie never gives
up on someone she likes and Thomas J is willing to help if he can.

IT was Thursday night and Harvey was worse. Now he wouldn't even speak to anyone. The nurses had started feeding him through a tube in his arm.

Harvey's father had come on Wednesday and sat with him for over an hour. He had told the doctors in a loud voice that money was no object. He told them they could spend whatever they had to and he would foot the bill. He said he had just gotten a contract to build an eight-unit town house.

"We're doing all we can now," one of the doctors had answered.

Carlie was furious when she heard about it. "You mean they let that rotten bum come in Harvey's room?"

"It's his father, Carlie."

"Whoo, next thing you know they'll be letting germs and viruses in."

That night when everyone was in bed at the Mason house, Carlie got up. She slipped into Thomas J's room and shone a flashlight in his face. "You asleep?"

He put his hand up to block out the light. "No, I was just lying here thinking."

"About Harvey?"

"Yeah. I'm used to him being on the bottom bunk and shifting around and all. I can't get to sleep without him. It's too quiet."

150

"Me either. Now, listen, I got an idea. You want to go in cahoots with me?"

Thomas J wasn't sure what that was, but he said, "I'd be glad to."

"All right, look, I went through the newspaper after supper and guess what I found in the ads!"

"What?"

"Look, it's right here." She shone the light on the folded newspaper. "Can you read it?"

Thomas J bent closer to the paper. Carlie was too impatient to wait for his eyes to focus. She read it herself. "Puppies free to good homes!"

"Puppies?"

"Yeah, Thomas J, we're going to go right over there first thing in the morning and get Harvey a puppy."

Thomas J couldn't seem to take it in. "A *puppy*?"

"Yeah, he's always wanted one — remember? It was the first thing on his list. And it'll cure him, Thomas J, I know it will. Why, if I was in the hospital half-dead and somebody hooked a floating opal around my neck, I'd get up and do the hula." She broke off. "And the best part is they're free. See? *Free* to good homes."

"But is this a good home?"

"If it's good enough for us, it's good enough for a dog, isn't it?"

"What about Mrs. Mason though? She might get mad."

"I'll take all the responsibility. I'm used to people being mad at me. It doesn't bother me a bit. I'll say I forced you to come with me and — "

"No, I want to come on my own. She can get mad at me too."

"All right then, after breakfast we'll go over to Woodland Circle — wherever that is — and we'll take a shopping bag — see, we'll have to sneak him into the hospital — and we'll pick out a puppy and take him over to the hospital and pull him out and sing 'Happy Birthday to You.' How does that sound?"

"It sounds good to me."

"I know it'll cure him. I mean, who is going to lie there staring up at the ceiling when a puppy is licking his face? It just can't be done."

"What if the puppy doesn't lick him though?"

"We'll pick one that will. After all, there're bound to be — how many puppies in a litter — six? Seven? There's bound to be one licker." At the door she paused and said, "Not a word of this to Mrs. Mason, you hear me?"

"Yes."

"Or Mr. Mason." Carlie sensed the bond that had grown between them.

There was a pause, then, "All right."

"See you in the morning."

Carlie and Thomas J walked slowly down the hospital hall with the shopping bag between them. "I wish he wasn't such a wiggler," Carlie said, looking straight ahead.

"That's why you picked him — because he was the liveliest one."

"I know, but I feel like we got a tiger in there, the way the bag's shaking. I'm afraid he's going to bust out the bottom."

"If he wets, I know he will."

"Don't even think such things," Carlie said. "And remember, every time you see a nurse, get in front of the bag. Nurses are known for their sharp eyes. Doctors aren't. We could bring an elephant in here and the doctors wouldn't notice."

Thomas J and Carlie went straight to Harvey's room. "Shut the door, shut the door," Carlie said quickly.

She ran over to Harvey's bed. He was staring at the ceiling. "Hey, it's just me, Carlie. You can look at me in safety. I'm not wearing one of my famous halters." He turned his eyes to her. "See, I lied." She grinned. "I've got on my shocking-pink one — your favorite." Before he could look back at the ceiling she said, "Hey, we brought you something."

Harvey didn't speak.

"And I'm not even going to make you guess what it is. I'm just going to tell you that it is fat, spotted, wiggly, that it has a tail and a pink nose and that it is dying to get out of this shopping bag." She reached down and brought up the puppy. "Taa-dah! Puppy-time!"

Carlie nudged Thomas J. "Happy Birthday to you, Happy Birthday to you, Happy Birthday dear Haaaaaarvey, Happy Birthday to you."

There was a silence. Thomas J said, "We wanted to get a white one so we could name him Snowball, but they all had spots on them."

Carlie set the puppy on the bed beside Harvey. She nudged him forward.

Delighted to be out of the bag, the puppy rushed for the nearest face — Harvey's — and began licking his neck.

Carlie looked at Thomas J and rolled her eyes upward. "Thank goodness," she mouthed.

Harvey didn't move. "Don't you like him, Harvey?" Thomas J asked. It was the first present he had ever been in on. He wanted more than anything that it be a success. "He's real nice — and fat too," Thomas J said. "Feel him."

"Yeah, pleasingly plump is not the word," Carlie said.

"And soft too," Thomas J said anxiously.

Harvey did not move. Thomas J squinted up at Carlie. "Should we sing the birthday song again?"

Suddenly Harvey lifted his hand. He laid it on the puppy.

"I don't think so." Carlie grinned.

Harvey spoke for the first time in two days. "Is this for me?" he asked.

"Compliments of Carlie and Thomas J," Carlie said.

"It's mine?"

"Yeah, it's your birthday present. We picked it out special."

"Permanently?"

"Sure, what kind of gifts do you think me and Thomas J give? If we'd wanted to give you something unpermanent we'd have gotten a Popsicle."

"I can keep him?"

"Yeah, sure, what else? As a matter of fact, he's unreturnable."

The puppy was wiggling against Harvey's neck, and suddenly Harvey started to cry. It was the first time he had cried since the accident. It was like the turning on of a spigot. He sobbed, and the tears rolled down his cheeks in streams. The puppy, wild with all the excitement, licked at the tears.

"Go ahead and cry all you want to," Carlie said happily. "You got your own personal crying towel now." She turned to Thomas J. "You know, when I get to be a nurse, every morning I'm going to bring a basket of puppies to the hospital with me. They're better than pills."

Harvey was still crying. "It just makes me feel so —" He broke off. "I don't know. It's just that I didn't think — oh, I don't know how I feel." He cried again.

The nurse on the floor was passing the door and heard the commotion. She stuck her head in the door.

"Under the covers, quick!" Carlie said, poking the puppy under the sheet.

"What's going on in here?"

"Believe it or not," Carlie said, "we are having a wonderful time."

The nurse kept looking at Harvey. She said, "Harvey, are you all right?"

"Yes'm."

"Are you laughing or crying?"

"Both, I guess."

The nurse kept standing there. She noticed the bulge under the sheet, but she decided to ignore it. This was the first time Harvey had shown any sign of life in two days. "You want anything?" she asked.

"No."

"Cokes," Carlie hissed at him.

"Oh, yeah, could me and my friends have a Coke?" Harvey asked. "It's my birthday." He wiped his remaining tears on the sheet.

"Of course."

"Want to see what I got for my birthday? My friends gave it to me."

"Don't —" Carlie started to say, but Harvey reached under the sheet and pulled out the puppy before she could finish.

"Now, you know better than to have a puppy in here," the nurse said. "Why, if I had seen that puppy I would have to send him out right this minute."

"Yes'm."

She smiled. "I'll bring the Cokes." She started out the door and then leaned back in. "And many happy returns of the day, Harvey."

"Thank you." As the door closed, he held up the puppy so he could get a good look now that his eyes were dry. "This is the nicest puppy I have ever seen."

"Thomas J and me only give the best," Carlie said.

"There was six of them," Thomas J said, "but this one came running over and started licking us and we knew it was the one for you."

Carlie said, "Listen, don't think this puppy is *all* you're getting for your birthday though. I'm making my famous mayonnaise cake and bringing it over tonight."

"And will you bring the puppy back then too?"

"Listen, this puppy is not so easy to lug around," Carlie said. "If you want to do any real playing with him, you're going to have to get out of this hospital."

"I will," Harvey said, "but will you bring him tonight?"

"*If*," Carlie said, "Mrs. Mason will lend me her tote bag."

LANGSTON HUGHES

MY PEOPLE

THE night is beautiful,
So the faces of my people.

The stars are beautiful,
So the eyes of my people.

Beautiful, also, is the sun,
Beautiful, also, are the souls of my people.

ALL KINDS OF ANIMALS

COYOTE AND WATER SERPENT

LONG time ago, when the earth was still young, Coyote and Water Serpent were the best of friends. They would drop by each other's house whenever it occurred to them to do so. Coyote and Water Serpent were young in those days and their story had not yet unfolded.

One morning after Water Serpent had finished his breakfast, he decided to visit his good friend Coyote. As he neared Coyote's house he could see smoke rising and knew his friend was at home.

"Hello," he shouted into Coyote's den, "Anyone home? May I come in to visit?"

"Of course," replied Coyote, being a friendly sort of fellow. "Come share the warmth of my fire and have a chat."

Water Serpent poked his head into Coyote's house and started to slide in. Now, although he had not yet reached his adult size, Water Serpent was a very big snake. He slid in one coil, which bumped up against each wall of the room, and it was not all of him. He slithered some more and another coil overlapped the first and it was not all of him. He slid and slithered and piled coil upon coil until Coyote was pushed to the very edge of his firepit. When Water Serpent was all the way in and comfortable, there was no room for Coyote. He was forced to sit, all scrunched up, close to the heat of the fire.

160

But Water Serpent was his friend and soon they began to gossip about what was happening in the village nearby and when the rains might start. All the while, Water Serpent seemed not to notice his friend's discomfort, and Coyote, being the sort that he was, fell to scheming and planning how he would get back at his friend.

Finally, Water Serpent announced his departure, saying, "Come to visit me soon. Don't stay away too long." And he began to leave. Unlike most other creatures, it took quite some time for him to emerge completely from Coyote's home, and he was still slithering out when Coyote settled upon his plan.

Coyote was so anxious to put his scheme in action that he rushed through his supper and ran out into the evening. Soon he came to a spot full of juniper trees. It was just what he was looking for. He stripped the bark from some trees, picked up some yucca leaves, and arrived back home with his arms laden.

Once inside, Coyote started working. He worked all night. By the time the morning sun crept into his den, he had fashioned a tail from the juniper bark and yucca leaves. It looked just like Water Serpent's tail and it was almost as long.

Coyote was very pleased with himself and with his plan, but the tail needed one last finishing touch so that Water Serpent would believe it was really Coyote's tail. He started pulling tufts of fur from his body and sticking them onto the tail, and soon indeed it looked just like the rest of him.

"I can't wait till it's time to visit Water Serpent," he thought to himself. "Then he'll know what it's like to be squashed and squeezed and made uncomfortable in your own home."

The next day Coyote and his new tail made their way over to Water Serpent's house.

"Anyone home?" he called out. "May I come in?"

"Of course. Come on in," answered Water Serpent, and Coyote proudly began his entrance.

"I don't know what's happening to me," he said to Water Serpent, "but all of a sudden I seem to have grown this very long tail. It's almost

as long as yours. I can't imagine where it came from. You'll have to excuse me if I take up more room than usual."

And, since Coyote thought he was going to teach Water Serpent a lesson, he, too, draped his tail around the whole room. Water Serpent had a big house, but soon he was crushed up against one side of the room, his coils in an uncomfortable knot. Coyote, appearing not to notice, began to talk. He talked all afternoon, enjoying his trick. But Water Serpent saw what Coyote was up to and knew that the tail wasn't a real one.

At suppertime Coyote took his leave, humming and thinking to himself that Water Serpent had fallen for his trick. He was very proud of himself. But Water Serpent was at home, thinking, "That Coyote, he's always up to something. He really thought I wouldn't notice that his tail was fake."

Soon it was Water Serpent's turn to visit. As he came near Coyote's house, Coyote quickly tied on his tail and went to the opening of his den to greet his friend.

Water Serpent said, "I think you should know that since we last met I've grown again. I'm not sure we'll both fit in your house anymore."

"Oh, I'm sure we will. Here, I'll come out and you go in first."

Water Serpent went in and in and in and in and in. There wasn't any room for Coyote after all. To be polite, he was forced to sit outside and entertain his friend from there. It was very chilly that day, and as Coyote grew colder and colder, he found himself wishing that his friend would go home.

But Water Serpent had no intention of leaving. He was quite happy to make his friend uncomfortable in retaliation for Coyote's last visit. So he stayed, and they chatted about this and that, and only when Coyote's teeth began to chatter did he say, "Well, I must be going now."

"If you insist," replied the shivering Coyote, who was already trying to push past Water Serpent's coils in his rush to get to the fire. By the time the last of Water Serpent's tail was finally out of his house, Coyote had already hatched another plan to get even.

That evening Coyote returned to the stand of junipers. He dragged even more bark and yucca back to his house than he had before. Once again he made the bark and yucca leaves ready for tail-making.

When he was finished, Coyote was sure he had the longest tail in the whole world. Certainly it was long enough to force Water Serpent to sit outside when he went to visit the next bitterly cold day.

So Coyote waited for a cold day. And waited. The weather turned unseasonably warm. Coyote was not very good at biding his time, but now he was patient. He knew the wait would be worth it.

The fourth day was bright and cold and just right for Coyote's visit. He got ready in a hurry and was soon at Water Serpent's house.

"Here I am at last," he called out. "It's been a long time since we visited. May I come in?"

"Of course. How nice to see you," replied Water Serpent.

"I should warn you," Coyote shouted into the house, "that since you last saw me, I, too, have grown quite a bit. There may not be room in your house for both of us."

And with that, Coyote began to drag his tail into Water Serpent's house. It was soon obvious that Coyote's tail would fill every nook and cranny in the house, and Water Serpent politely offered to take his turn sitting outside.

"Oh no, you mustn't on my account," said Coyote. "You'll catch your death of cold."

"It's not that chilly," responded Water Serpent. "I'll be fine."

And so they idled the day away talking of things near and far. Water Serpent grew colder and colder and he, too, began to wish that his friend would go home.

But Coyote was enjoying his revenge and he was not about to cut his visit short. Water Serpent was so cold he thought his eyes would turn to ice. He was so cold his nose began to run. He thought Coyote would never leave.

As the sun began to set, Coyote finally roused himself from his place next to Water Serpent's cozy fire and announced his departure. When he disappeared into the distance over a small hill and his tail was still leaving Water Serpent's house, Water Serpent thought, "This is getting out of hand. I'm going to have to do something to end this silly competition. Coyote will never stop. He's a petty, vengeful wretch. He made me almost freeze to death!"

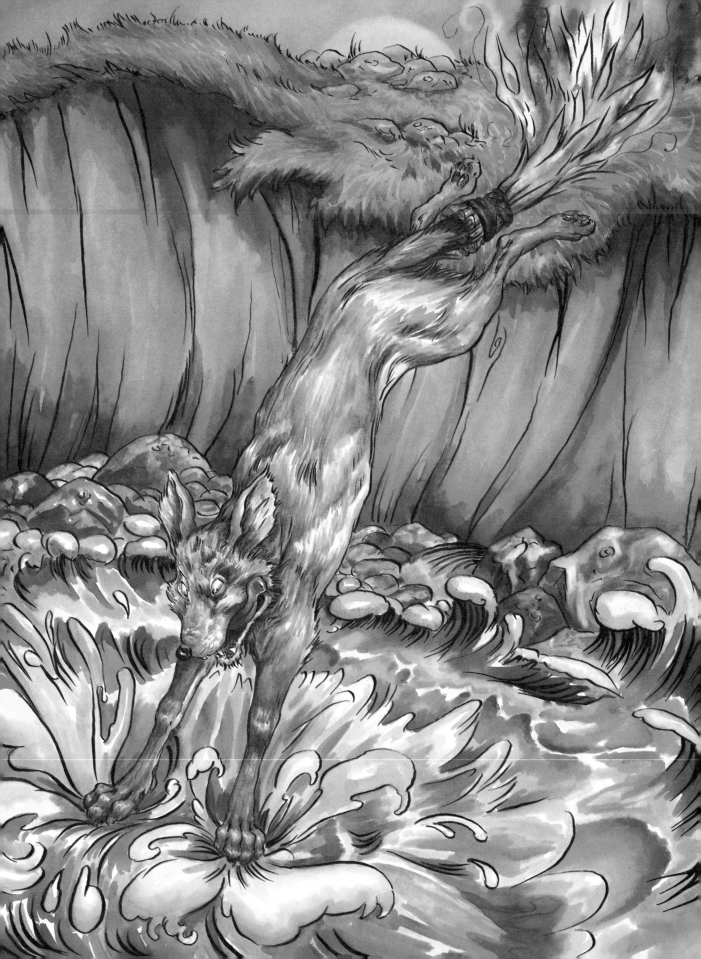

At just that moment, the last of Coyote's tail brushed past the fire and the angry Water Serpent knew what he was going to do. He grabbed the end of the tail and stuck it in the fire.

Meanwhile, Coyote had topped another rise. He was so in love with his tail that he felt he just had to turn around and admire it again. In doing so, he noticed a fire way off in the distance and thought that a brush fire had started near Water Serpent's house. But when Coyote looked again, the fire seemed to be following him. He thought men were perhaps having a coyote drive and that it would be unwise to return to his house just yet.

So Coyote veered off in a new direction. His walk became a trot; his trot a run. Everywhere he looked there seemed to be brush fires now. He was unaware that the swishing of his own tail had started the fires. He was only conscious that they seemed to be catching up to him. The faster he ran, the more the sparks flew from his burning tail and set ablaze the dry grasses.

Coyote, in a panic now, thought only of reaching the river. He had no idea that he was being chased by his own burning tail. He was certain that unknown enemies were hunting him down, beating him out of cover with the use of fire.

But as he approached the river, Coyote took one last look behind him. The fire had reached him, and he at last realized that he had been running away from his own tail. He jumped into the river and was never seen again.

When Coyote did not return, Water Serpent was not a bit upset. "Served him right," he muttered to himself. "Coyote could never leave well enough alone. Always making trouble and scheming. Now he'll not bother us again."

And so Water Serpent lost his best friend. Who knows, he may be alone still.

CUNNING BRER RABBIT

NE day Brer Bear decided to set out and dig himself a store of peanuts for the winter. Brer Rabbit, hiding in the bushes, saw Brer Bear with his donkey and his cart and heard him calling out to his missus that he would be back at the end of the day with a cartload of the best peanuts around.

Brer Rabbit thought to himself that he and his missus needed a pile of peanuts for the winter, too. And Brer Rabbit wasn't one to do a lot of work if he thought he could get someone else to do it for him.

So he rooted around his burrow and found a red kerchief that he wrapped around his neck. He tied it tightly, ran out to where Brer Bear would be passing by, and lay down in the middle of the road.

Brer Bear spent a very busy day gathering nuts and was coming home with a full cart when he saw Brer Rabbit lying in the road.

"Why, that looks like Brer Rabbit dead in the road with his throat cut wide open," said Brer Bear. "Mm-mh. The missus sure will be happy when I tell her I've got peanuts and a rabbit for rabbit stew."

Brer Bear got down from his cart, picked up Brer Rabbit and threw him in the back with the load of peanuts. No sooner was Brer Bear's back turned than Brer Rabbit sprang up and jumped out of the cart with Brer Bear's entire load of peanuts.

Brer Bear didn't notice a thing.

Brer Bear pulled up to the tree where he and Missus Bear had set up house and called out, "Come on out, Missus. It was a great day. Peanuts here; rabbit there."

Missus Bear shuffled out and looked in the cart where she could see only a few peanuts rolling around. She scratched her head, looked grumpily around and said, "Peanuts gone; rabbit, too."

The following day, Brer Bear started out again. "Don't lose those peanuts today. It's getting late in the year," Missus Bear called out.

Meanwhile, Brer Fox, who had been lurking in the bushes and had seen Brer Rabbit's trick, decided that a good trick was worth repeating.

"I'll do the same thing," he said to himself and went looking for a red kerchief he could tie around his neck.

Brer Fox wasn't nearly as smart as everyone thought, though. He went right to the very same place in the road where Brer Bear had

found Brer Rabbit. He lay down just like Brer Rabbit had and waited.

A little while later, Brer Bear came around that corner in the road and saw Brer Fox lying there.

"Why, there's that thief from yesterday. Looks like somebody done run him over but good this time. Missus Bear will have meat stew for sure today."

Saying this, he climbed down and lifted up Brer Fox. "Oh boy," thought Brer Fox to himself. "Here come my peanuts."

But instead of throwing Brer Fox into the back of the cart, Brer Bear swung him around and bashed him against the cart's wheel.

"You look mighty dead to me," Brer Bear muttered to himself, "but today I'm just going to make sure."

Poor Brer Fox just barely managed to escape Brer Bear's licking.

It just goes to show that you can't get away with the same trick twice.

W ALLACE W ADSWORTH

THE WONDERFUL OX

There are many tall tales about the mighty logger Paul Bunyan,
but none more remarkable than those about Babe, Paul's gigantic blue ox.

T HE Great Blue Ox was so strong that he could pull anything that had two ends and some things that had no ends at all, which made him very valuable at times, as one can easily understand.

Babe was remarkable in a number of ways besides that of his color, which was a bright blue. His size is rather a matter of doubt, some people holding that he was twenty-four ax-handles and a plug of tobacco wide between the eyes, and others saying that he was forty-two ax-handles across the forehead. It may be that both are wrong, for the story goes that Jim, the pet crow, who always roosted on Babe's left horn, one day decided to fly across to the tip of the other horn. He got lost on the way, and didn't get to the other horn until after the spring thaw, and he had started in the dead of winter.

The Great Blue Ox was so long in the body that an ordinary person, standing at his head, would have had to use a pair of field glasses in order to see what the animal was doing with his hind feet.

Babe had a great love for Paul, and a peculiar way of showing it which discovered the great logger's only weakness. Paul was ticklish, especially around the neck, and the Ox had a strong passion for licking him there with his tongue. His master good-naturedly avoided such outbursts of affection from his pet whenever possible.

One day Paul took the Blue Ox with him to town, and there he

loaded him with all the supplies that would be needed for the camp and crew during the winter. When everything had been packed on Babe's back, the animal was so heavily laden that on the way back to camp he sank to his knees in the solid rock at nearly every step. These footprints later filled with water and became the countless lakes which are to be found to-day scattered throughout the state of Maine.

Babe was compelled to go slowly, of course, on account of the great load he carried, and so Paul had to camp overnight along the way. He took the packs from the Ox's back, turned the big animal out to graze, and after eating supper he and Ole lay down to sleep.

The Blue Ox, however, was for some strange reason in a restless mood that night, and after feeding all that he cared to, he wandered away for many miles before he finally found a place that suited his particular idea of what a bedding ground should be. There he lay down, and it is quite possible that he was very much amused in thinking of the trouble which his master would have in finding him the next morning. The Ox was a very wise creature, and every now and then he liked to play a little joke on Paul.

Along about dawn Paul Bunyan awoke and looked about for his pet. Not a glimpse of him could he get in any direction, though he whistled so loudly for him that the near-by trees were shattered into bits. At last, after he and Ole had eaten their breakfast and Babe still did not appear, Paul knew that the joke was on him. "He thinks he has put up a little trick on me," he said to Ole with a grin. "You go ahead and make up the packs again, while I play hide-and-seek for a while," and as the Big Swede started gathering everything together again he set off trailing the missing animal.

Babe's tracks were so large that it took three men, standing close together, to see across one of them, and they were so far apart that no one could follow them but Paul, who was an expert trailer, no one else ever being able to equal him in this ability. So remarkable was he in this respect that he could follow any tracks that were ever made, no matter how old or how faint they were. It is told of him that he once came across the carcass of a bull moose that had died of old age, and having a couple of hours to spare, and being also of an inquiring turn of mind, he followed the tracks of the moose back to the place where it had been born.

Being such an expert, therefore, it did not take him very long to locate Babe. The Great Blue Ox, when he at last came across him, was lying down contentedly chewing his cud, and waiting for his master to come and find him. "You worthless critter!" Paul said to him, and thwacked him good-naturedly with his hand. "Look at the trouble you have put me to, and just look at the damage you have done here," and he pointed to the great hollow place in the ground which Babe had wallowed out while lying there. The Ox's only reply was to smother Paul for a moment with a loving, juicy lick of his great tongue, and then together they set off to where Ole was waiting for them.

Any one, by looking at a map of the state of Maine, can easily locate Moosehead Lake, which is, as history shows, the place where the Great Blue Ox lay down.

No one, certainly, could be expected to copy him in the matter of straightening out crooked logging trails. It was all wild country where Paul did his logging, and about the only roads which he found through the woods were the trails and paths made by the wild animals that had traveled over them for hundreds of years. Paul decided to use these game trails as logging roads, but they twisted and turned in every direction and were all so crooked that they had to be straightened before any use could be made of them. It is well known that the Great Blue Ox was so powerful that he could pull anything that had two ends, and so when Paul wanted a crooked logging trail straightened out, he would just hitch Babe up to one end of it, tell his pet to go ahead, and, lo and behold! the crooked trail would be pulled out perfectly straight.

There was one particularly bad stretch of road, about twenty or thirty miles long, that gave Babe and Paul a lot of trouble before they finally got all the crooks pulled out of it. It certainly must have been the crookedest road in the world — it twisted and turned so much that it spelled out every letter of the alphabet, some of the letters two or three times. Paul taught Babe how to read just by leading him over it a few times, and men going along it met themselves coming from the other

direction so often that the whole camp was near crazy before long.

So Paul decided that the road would have to be straightened out without any further delay, and with that end in view he ordered Ole to make for him the strongest chain he knew how. The Big Swede set to work with a will, and when the chain was completed it had links four feet long and two feet across and the steel they were made of was thirteen inches thick.

The chain being ready, Paul hitched Babe up to one end of the road with it. At his master's word the Great Blue Ox began to puff and pull and strain away as he had never done before, and at last he got the end pulled out a little ways. Paul chirped to him again, and he pulled away harder than ever. With every tug he made one of the twists in the road would straighten out, and then Babe would pull away again, hind legs straight out behind and belly to the ground. It was the hardest job Babe had ever been put up against, but he stuck to it most admirably.

When the task was finally done the Ox was nearly fagged out, a condition that he had never known before, and that big chain had been pulled on so hard that it was pulled out into a solid steel bar. The road was straightened out, however, which was the thing Paul wanted, and he considered the time and energy expended as well worth while, since the nuisance had been transformed into something useful. He found, though, that since all the kinks and twists had been pulled out, there was now a whole lot more of the road than was needed, but — never being a person who could stand to waste anything which might be useful — he rolled up all the extra length and laid it down in a place where there had never been a road before but where one might come in handy some time.

Nor was the straightening of crooked roads the only useful work which the Great Blue Ox did. It was also his task to skid or drag the logs from the stumps to the rollways by the streams, where they were stored for the drives. Babe was always obedient, and a tireless and patient worker. It is said that the timber of nineteen states, except a few scant sections here and there which Paul Bunyan did not touch, was skidded from the stumps by the all-powerful Great Blue Ox. He was docile and willing, and could be depended upon for the performance of almost any task set him, except that once in a while he would develop a sudden streak of mischief and drink a river dry behind a drive or run off into the woods. Sometimes he would step on a ridge that formed the bank of the river, and smash it down so that the river would start running out through his tracks, thus changing its course entirely from what Paul had counted on.

ROBERT FROST

THE RUNAWAY

NCE when the snow of the year was beginning to fall,
We stopped by a mountain pasture to say, "Whose colt?"
A little Morgan had one forefoot on the wall,
The other curled at his breast. He dipped his head
And snorted at us. And then he had to bolt.
We heard the miniature thunder where he fled,
And we saw him, or thought we saw him, dim and gray,
Like a shadow against the curtain of falling flakes.
"I think the little fellow's afraid of the snow.
He isn't winter-broken. It isn't play
With the little fellow at all. He's running away.
I doubt if even his mother could tell him, 'Sakes,
It's only weather.' He'd think she didn't know!
Where is his mother? He can't be out alone."
And now he comes again with clatter of stone,
And mounts the wall again with whited eyes
And all his tail that isn't hair up straight.
He shudders his coat as if to throw off flies.
"Whoever it is that leaves him out so late,
When other creatures have gone to stall and bin,
Ought to be told to come and take him in."

BEVERLY CLEARY

HENRY AND RIBS

"Henry and Ribs" is the first chapter of Henry Huggins,
one of Beverly Cleary's best-loved books since its publication in 1950.

ENRY Huggins was in the third grade. His hair looked like a scrubbing brush and most of his grown-up front teeth were in. He lived with his mother and father in a square white house on Klickitat Street. Except for having his tonsils out when he was six and breaking his arm falling out of a cherry tree when he was seven, nothing much happened to Henry.

I wish something exciting would happen, Henry often thought.

But nothing very interesting ever happened to Henry, at least not until one Wednesday afternoon in March. Every Wednesday after school Henry rode downtown on the bus to go swimming at the Y.M.C.A. After he swam for an hour, he got on the bus again and rode home just in time for dinner. It was fun but not really exciting.

When Henry left the Y.M.C.A. on this particular Wednesday, he stopped to watch a man tear down a circus poster. Then, with three nickels and one dime in his pocket, he went to the corner drugstore to buy a chocolate ice cream cone. He thought he would eat the ice cream cone, get on the bus, drop his dime in the slot, and ride home.

That is not what happened.

He bought the ice cream cone and paid for it with one of his nickels. On his way out of the drugstore he stopped to look at funny books. It was a free look, because he had only two nickels left.

He stood there licking his chocolate ice cream cone and reading one of the funny books when he heard a thump, thump, thump. Henry turned, and there behind him was a dog. The dog was scratching himself. He wasn't any special kind of dog. He was too small to be a big dog but, on the other hand, he was much too big to be a little dog. He wasn't a white dog, because parts of him were brown and other parts were black and in between there were yellowish patches. His ears stood up and his tail was long and thin.

The dog was hungry. When Henry licked, he licked. When Henry swallowed, he swallowed.

"Hello, you old dog," Henry said. "You can't have my ice cream cone."

Swish, swish, swish went the tail. "Just one bite," the dog's brown eyes seemed to say.

"Go away," ordered Henry. He wasn't very firm about it. He patted the dog's head.

The tail wagged harder. Henry took one last lick. "Oh, all right," he said. "If you're that hungry, you might as well have it."

The ice cream cone disappeared in one gulp.

"Now go away," Henry told the dog. "I have to catch a bus for home."

He started for the door. The dog started, too.

"Go away, you skinny old dog." Henry didn't say it very loudly. "Go on home."

The dog sat down at Henry's feet. Henry looked at the dog and the dog looked at Henry.

"I don't think you've got a home. You're awful thin. Your ribs show right through your skin."

Thump, thump, thump replied the tail.

"And you haven't got a collar," said Henry.

He began to think. If only he could keep the dog! He had always wanted a dog of his very own and now he had found a dog that wanted him. He couldn't go home and leave a hungry dog on the street corner. If only he knew what his mother and father would say! He fingered the

two nickels in his pocket. That was it! He would use one of the nickels to phone his mother.

"Come on, Ribsy. Come on, Ribs, old boy. I'm going to call you Ribsy because you're so thin."

The dog trotted after the boy to the telephone booth in the corner of the drugstore. Henry shoved him into the booth and shut the door. He had never used a pay telephone before. He had to put the telephone book on the floor and stand on tiptoe on it to reach the mouthpiece. He gave the operator his number and dropped his nickel into the coin box.

"Hello — Mom?"

"Why, Henry!" His mother sounded surprised. "Where are you?"

"At the drugstore near the Y."

Ribs began to scratch. Thump, thump, thump. Inside the telephone booth the thumps sounded loud and hollow.

"For goodness' sake, Henry, what's that noise?" his mother demanded. Ribs began to whimper and then to howl. "Henry," Mrs. Huggins shouted, "are you all right?"

"Yes, I'm all right," Henry shouted back. He never could understand why his mother always thought something had happened to him when nothing ever did. "That's just Ribsy."

"Ribsy?" His mother was exasperated. "Henry, will you please tell me what is going on?"

"I'm trying to," said Henry. Ribsy howled louder. People were gathering around the phone booth to see what was going on. "Mother, I've found a dog. I sure wish I could keep him. He's a good dog and I'd feed him and wash him and everything. Please, Mom."

"I don't know, dear," his mother said. "You'll have to ask your father."

"Mom!" Henry wailed. "That's what you always say!" Henry was tired of standing on tiptoe and the phone booth was getting warm. "Mom, please say yes and I'll never ask for another thing as long as I live!"

"Well, all right, Henry. I guess there isn't any reason why you shouldn't have a dog. But you'll have to bring him home on the bus. Your father has the car today and I can't come after you. Can you manage?"

"Sure! Easy."

"And Henry, please don't be late. It looks as if it might rain."

"All right, Mom." Thump, thump, thump.

"Henry, what's that thumping noise?"

"It's my dog, Ribsy. He's scratching a flea."

"Oh, Henry," Mrs. Huggins moaned. "Couldn't you have found a dog without fleas?"

Henry thought that was a good time to hang up. "Come on, Ribs," he said. "We're going home on the bus."

When the big green bus stopped in front of the drugstore, Henry picked up his dog. Ribsy was heavier than he expected. He had a hard time getting him into the bus and was wondering how he would get a dime out of his pocket when the driver said, "Say, sonny, you can't take that dog on the bus."

"Why not?" asked Henry.

"It's a company rule, sonny. No dogs on buses."

"Golly, Mister, how'm I going to get him home? I just have to get him home."

"Sorry, sonny. I didn't make the rule. No animal can ride on a bus unless it's inside a box."

"Well, thanks anyway," said Henry doubtfully, and lifted Ribsy off the bus.

"Well, I guess we'll have to get a box. I'll get you onto the next bus somehow," promised Henry.

He went back into the drugstore followed closely by Ribsy. "Have you got a big box I could have, please?" he asked the man at the tooth-paste counter. "I need one big enough for my dog."

The clerk leaned over the counter to look at Ribsy. "A cardboard box?" he asked.

"Yes, please," said Henry, wishing the man would hurry. He didn't want to be late getting home.

The clerk pulled a box out from under the counter. "This hair tonic carton is the only one I have. I guess it's big enough, but why anyone would want to put a dog in a cardboard box I can't understand."

The box was about two feet square and six inches deep. On one end was printed, "Don't Let Them Call You Baldy," and on the other, "Try Our Large Economy Size."

Henry thanked the clerk, carried the box out to the bus stop, and put it on the sidewalk. Ribsy padded after him. "Get in, fellow," Henry commanded. Ribsy understood. He stepped into the box and sat down just as the bus came around the corner. Henry had to kneel to pick up the box. It was not a very strong box and he had to put his arms under it. He staggered as he lifted it, feeling like the strong man who lifted weights at the circus. Ribsy lovingly licked his face with his wet pink tongue.

"Hey, cut that out!" Henry ordered. "You better be good if you're going to ride on the bus with me."

The bus stopped at the curb. When it was Henry's turn to get on, he had trouble finding the step because he couldn't see his feet. He had to try several times before he hit it. Then he discovered he had forgotten

BEVERLY CLEARY

to take his dime out of his pocket. He was afraid to put the box down for fear Ribsy might escape.

He turned sideways to the driver and asked politely, "Will you please take the dime out of my pocket for me? My hands are full."

The driver pushed his cap back on his head and exclaimed, "Full! I should say they are full! And just where do you think you're going with that animal?"

"Home," said Henry in a small voice.

The passengers were staring and most of them were smiling. The box was getting heavier every minute.

"Not on this bus, you're not!" said the driver.

"But the man on the last bus said I could take the dog on the bus in a box," protested Henry, who was afraid he couldn't hold the dog much longer. "He said it was a company rule."

"He meant a big box tied shut. A box with holes punched in it for the dog to breathe through."

Henry was horrified to hear Ribsy growl. "Shut up," he ordered.

Ribsy began to scratch his left ear with his left hind foot. The box began to tear. Ribsy jumped out of the box and off the bus and Henry jumped after him. The bus pulled away with a puff of exhaust.

"Now see what you've done! You've spoiled everything." The dog hung his head and tucked his tail between his legs. "If I can't get you home, how can I keep you?"

Henry sat down on the curb to think. It was so late and the clouds were so dark that he didn't want to waste time looking for a big box. His mother was probably beginning to worry about him.

People were stopping on the corner to wait for the next bus. Among them Henry noticed an elderly lady carrying a large paper shopping bag full of apples. The shopping bag gave him an idea. Jumping up, he snapped his fingers at Ribs and ran back into the drugstore.

"You back again?" asked the toothpaste clerk. "What do you want this time? String and paper to wrap your dog in?"

"No, sir," said Henry. "I want one of those big nickel shopping bags." He laid his last nickel on the counter.

"Well, I'll be darned," said the clerk, and handed the bag across the counter.

Henry opened the bag, and set it up on the floor. He picked up Ribsy and shoved him hind feet first into the bag. Then he pushed his front feet in. A lot of Ribsy was left over.

The clerk was leaning over the counter watching. "I guess I'll have to have some string and paper, too," Henry said, "if I can have some free."

"Well! Now I've seen everything." The clerk shook his head as he handed a piece of string and a big sheet of paper across the counter.

Ribsy whimpered, but he held still while Henry wrapped the paper loosely around his head and shoulders and tied it with the string. The dog made a lumpy package, but by taking one handle of the bag in each

hand Henry was able to carry it to the bus stop. He didn't think the bus driver would notice him. It was getting dark and a crowd of people, most of them with packages, was waiting on the corner. A few spatters of rain hit the pavement.

This time Henry remembered his dime. Both hands were full, so he held the dime in his teeth and stood behind the woman with the bag of apples. Ribsy wiggled and whined, even though Henry tried to pet him through the paper. When the bus stopped, he climbed on behind the lady, quickly set the bag down, dropped his dime in the slot, picked up the bag, and squirmed through the crowd to a seat beside a fat man near the back of the bus.

"Whew!" Henry sighed with relief. The driver was the same one he had met on the first bus! But Ribs was on the bus at last. Now if he could only keep him quiet for fifteen minutes they would be home and Ribsy would be his for keeps.

The next time the bus stopped Henry saw Scooter McCarthy, a fifth grader at school, get on and make his way through the crowd to the back of the bus.

Just my luck, thought Henry. I'll bet he wants to know what's in my bag.

"Hi," said Scooter.

"Hi," said Henry.

"Whatcha got in that bag?" asked Scooter.

"None of your beeswax," answered Henry.

Scooter looked at Henry. Henry looked at Scooter. Crackle, crackle, crackle went the bag. Henry tried to hold it more tightly between his knees.

"There's something alive in that bag!" Scooter said accusingly.

"Shut up, Scooter!" whispered Henry.

"Aw, shut up yourself!" said Scooter. "You've got something alive in that bag!"

By this time the passengers at the back of the bus were staring at Henry and his package. Crackle, crackle, crackle. Henry tried to pat Ribsy again through the paper. The bag crackled even louder. Then it began to wiggle.

"Come on, tell us what's in the bag," coaxed the fat man.

"N-n-n-nothing," stammered Henry. "Just something I found."

"Maybe it's a rabbit," suggested one passenger. "I think it's kicking."

"No; it's too big for a rabbit," said another.

"I'll bet it's a baby," said Scooter. "I'll bet you kidnaped a baby!"

"I did not!"

Ribs began to whimper and then to howl. Crackle, crackle, crackle. Thump, thump, thump. Ribsy scratched his way out of the bag.

"Well, I'll be doggoned!" exclaimed the fat man and began to laugh. "I'll be doggoned!"

"It's just a skinny old dog," said Scooter.

"He is not! He's a good dog."

Henry tried to keep Ribsy between his knees. The bus lurched around a corner and started to go uphill. Henry was thrown against the fat man. The frightened dog wiggled away from him, squirmed between the passengers, and started for the front of the bus.

"Here, Ribsy, old boy! Come back here," called Henry and started after him.

"E-e-ek! A dog!" squealed the lady with the bag of apples. "Go away, doggie, go away!"

Ribsy was scared. He tried to run and crashed into the lady's bag of apples. The bag tipped over and the apples began to roll toward the back of the bus, which was grinding up a steep hill. The apples rolled around the feet of the people who were standing. Passengers began to slip and slide. They dropped their packages and grabbed one another.

Crash! A high-school girl dropped an armload of books.

Rattle! Bang! Crash! A lady dropped a big paper bag. The bag broke open and pots and pans rolled out.

Thud! A man dropped a coil of garden hose. The hose unrolled and the passengers found it wound around their legs.

People were sitting on the floor. They were sitting on books and apples. They were even sitting on other people's laps. Some of them had their hats over their faces and their feet in the air.

Skree-e-etch! The driver threw on the brakes and turned around in his seat just as Henry made his way through the apples and books and pans and hose to catch Ribsy.

The driver pushed his cap back on his head. "O.K., sonny," he said to Henry. "Now you know why dogs aren't allowed on buses!"

"Yes, sir," said Henry in a small voice. "I'm sorry."

"You're sorry! A lot of good that does. Look at this bus! Look at those people!"

"I didn't mean to make any trouble," said Henry. "My mother said I could keep the dog if I could bring him home on the bus."

The fat man began to snicker. Then he chuckled. Then he laughed

189

and then he roared. He laughed until tears streamed down his cheeks and all the other passengers were laughing too, even the man with the hose and the lady with the apples.

The driver didn't laugh. "Take that dog and get off the bus!" he ordered. Ribsy whimpered and tucked his tail between his legs.

The fat man stopped laughing. "See here, driver," he said, "you can't put that boy and his dog off in the rain."

"Well, he can't stay on the bus," snapped the driver.

Henry didn't know what he was going to do. He guessed he'd have to walk the rest of the way home. He wasn't sure he knew the way in the dark.

Just then a siren screamed. It grew louder and louder until it stopped right alongside the bus.

A policeman appeared in the entrance. "Is there a boy called Henry Huggins on this bus?" he asked.

"Oh boy, you're going to be arrested for having a dog on the bus!" gloated Scooter. "I'll bet you have to go to jail!"

"I'm him," said Henry in a very small voice.

"I am he," corrected the lady with the apples, who had been a schoolteacher and couldn't help correcting boys.

"You'd better come along with us," said the policeman.

"Boy, you're sure going to get it!" said Scooter.

"Surely going to get it," corrected the apple lady.

Henry and Ribsy followed the policeman off the bus and into the squad car, where Henry and the dog sat in the back seat.

"Are you going to arrest me?" Henry asked timidly.

"Well, I don't know. Do you think you ought to be arrested?"

"No, sir," said Henry politely. He thought the policeman was joking, but he wasn't sure. It was hard to tell about grownups sometimes. "I didn't mean to do anything. I just had to get Ribsy home. My mother said I could keep him if I could bring him home on the bus."

"What do you think?" the officer asked his partner, who was driving the squad car.

"We-e-ell, I think we might let him off this time," answered the

driver. "His mother must be pretty worried about him if she called the police, and I don't think she'd want him to go to jail."

"Yes, he's late for his dinner already. Let's see how fast we can get him home."

The driver pushed a button and the siren began to shriek. Ribsy raised his head and howled. The tires sucked at the wet pavement and the windshield wipers splip-splopped. Henry began to enjoy himself. Wouldn't this be something to tell the kids at school! Automobiles pulled over to the curb as the police car went faster and faster. Even the bus Henry had been on had to pull over and stop. Henry waved to the passengers. They waved back. Up the hill the police car sped and around

the corner until they came to Klickitat Street and then to Henry's block and then pulled up in front of his house.

Henry's mother and father were standing on the porch waiting for him. The neighbors were looking out of their windows.

"Well!" said his father after the policeman had gone. "It's about time you came home. So this is Ribsy! I've heard about you, fellow, and there's a big bone and a can of Feeley's Flea Flakes waiting for you."

"Henry, what *will* you do next?" sighed his mother.

"Golly, Mom, I didn't do anything. I just brought my dog home on the bus like you said."

Ribsy sat down and began to scratch.

THE ISLAND

Alec Ramsay is having a rather dull voyage home from a visit to India
until the ship puts in at an Arab port and takes aboard a wild desert stallion.
Alec is fascinated by this beautiful, untamed horse. When the ship begins to sink
in a gale, he frees the horse so that it can save itself, but it is the horse that saves
Alec by pulling him through the raging sea to a deserted island.

LEC opened his eyes. The sun, high in the heavens, beat down upon his bare head. His face felt hot, his tongue swollen. Slowly he pushed his tired body from the ground and then fell back upon the sand. He lay still a few moments. Then he gathered himself and once again attempted to rise. Wearily he got to his knees, then to his feet. His legs trembled beneath him. He unbuckled the battered life jacket and let it fall to the ground.

He looked around; he needed water desperately. He saw the Black's hoof marks in the sand. Perhaps, if he followed them, they would lead him to fresh water; he was sure that the stallion was as thirsty as he. Alec stumbled along. The hoof marks turned abruptly away from the ocean toward the interior of the island. There was no sign of vegetation around him — only hot sand. He turned and looked back at the now calm and peaceful sea. So much had happened in such a short space of time! What had happened to the others? Was he the only one who had survived?

A few minutes later he turned and made his way up a high sand dune. At the crest he stopped. From where he stood he could see the entire island; it was small — not more than two miles in circumference. It seemed barren except for a few trees, bushes and scattered patches of burned grass. High rock cliffs dropped down to the sea on the other side of the island.

The Black's hoof marks led down the hill, and a short distance away beneath a few scattered trees, Alec saw a small spring-water pool. His swollen tongue ran across cracked lips as he stumbled forward. To the right of the spring, a hundred yards away, he saw the Black — hungrily feasting upon the dry grass. Alec again saw that small Arabian port and the crowd gathered around the prone figure of the Arab whom the Black had struck. Would he be safe from the stallion?

The Black looked up from his grazing. The boy noticed that the horse had torn or slipped off his halter somehow. The wind whipped through his mane; his smooth black body was brilliant in the sun. He saw Alec, and his shrill whistle echoed through the air. He reared, his front legs striking out. Then he came down, and his right foreleg pawed into the dirt.

Alec looked around him. There was no place to seek cover. He was too weak to run, even if there was. His gaze returned to the stallion, fascinated by a creature so wild and so near. Here was the wildest of all wild animals — he had fought for everything he had ever needed, for food, for leadership, for life itself; it was his nature to kill or be killed. The horse reared again; then he snorted and plunged straight for the boy.

Alec didn't move. His body was numb. Hypnotized, he watched the stallion coming. Then, twenty-five yards from him, the Black stopped. The whites of his eyes gleamed, his nostrils curled, his ears were back flat against his head. He whistled shrill, clear and long. Suddenly he moved between Alec and the spring. He pawed furiously at the earth.

Alec stood still, not daring to move. After what seemed hours, the stallion stopped tearing up the earth. His gaze turned from the boy to the pool and then back again. He whistled, half-reared, and then broke into his long stride, running back in the direction from which he had come.

Alec forced his legs into action, reached the spring and threw himself on the ground beside it. He let his face fall into the cool, clear water. It seemed that he would never get enough; he doused his head, and let the water run down his back. Then he tore off part of his shirt

196

and bathed his skinned body. Refreshed, he crawled beneath the shaded bushes growing beside the pool. He stretched out, closed his eyes and fell asleep, exhausted.

Only once during the night did Alec stir; sleepily he opened his eyes. He could see the moon through the bushes, high above the star-studded sky. A big, black figure moved by the spring — the Black, and only a few feet away! He drank deeply and then raised his beautiful head, his ears pricked forward; he turned and trotted away.

Alec awoke very hungry the next morning. He had gone a day and a half without eating! He rose and drank from the spring. The next thing was to find food. He walked for quite some distance before he found anything edible. It was a berry bush; the fruit was unlike that of anything he had ever tasted before. But he might not easily find anything else that he could eat, so he made a meal of berries.

Then he explored the island. He found it to be flat between the sand dune that he had climbed the day before and the rocky cliffs of the other side of the island. He made no attempt to climb over the large boulders. There were few berry bushes and little grass, and Alec realized that food would be scarce for him and the Black. The island seemed to be totally uninhabited. He had seen no birds or animals of any kind.

He walked slowly back in the direction of the spring. From the top of the hill he looked out upon the open sea, hoping desperately that he would see a boat. Only the vast expanse of blue water spread before him. Below he saw the Black cantering along the beach. Alec forgot his problems in the beauty of the stallion as he swept along, graceful in his swift stride, his black mane and tail flying. When the horse vanished around the bend of the island, Alec walked down to the beach.

The next thing that he must do was to erect some sort of a shelter for himself; and first he must find driftwood. Alec's eyes swept the shore. He saw one piece, then another.

For the next few hours he struggled with the wood that he found cast upon the beach, dragging it back toward the spring. He piled it up and was surprised to see how much he had gathered. He looked for a long, heavy piece and found one that suited his purpose. He pulled it toward two adjoining scrub trees and hoisted it between the two crotches. Suddenly his arms shook and he stopped. Painted on the gray board was the name DRAKE — it had been part of one of the lifeboats! Alec stood still a moment, then grimly he fixed the plank securely in place.

Next he leaned the remaining pieces of wood on each side of the plank, making a shelter in the form of a tent. He filled in the open ends as well as he could. With his knife he skinned the bark from a tree and tied the pieces of wood together.

Alec went back to the beach and gathered all the seaweed that he could carry. He stuffed this into all the open holes. He surveyed his finished shelter — he was afraid a good wind would blow it down on top of him!

He looked up at the hot sun and guessed it to be near noon. His skin and clothes were wet with perspiration from the terrific heat. He cut a long, slender staff from a tree, tested it and found it to be strong. Carefully he skinned it and cut it the right length. Then he tied his knife securely to the end of the stick with a piece of bark.

A short time later Alec stood beside a small cove which he had discovered that morning. The water was clear and the sand glistened white beneath it. He seated himself upon the bank and peered eagerly into the water. He had read of people catching fish this way. After some time he saw a ripple. Carefully he raised his improvised spear. Then Alec flung it with all his might; the long stick whizzed down into the water and pierced its way into the white sand. He had missed!

He pulled his spear out and moved to another spot. Again he waited patiently. It was a long time before he saw another fish. A long slender shape moved in the shallow water beneath him. He raised his spear, took aim and plunged again. He saw the knife hit! Fearing the knife would slip out of the fish if he pulled the spear up, he jumped into the shallow water and shoved it against the bottom. Desperately Alec's arm flew down the stick, seeking the fish. The water was churned with sand. He came to the end, only the steel blade met his searching fingers. He had lost it!

For the rest of the afternoon, Alec strove to catch a fish. As darkness fell, he rose wearily to his feet and walked slowly back to his new "home." His eyes ached from the hours of strain of constant searching into the depths of the water.

On his way, he stopped at the berry bush and ate hungrily. When he reached the spring, he saw the Black not far away. He looked up, saw the boy and continued to eat. Moving from one place to another, he tore away at the small patches of grass that he could find. "I'll bet he's as hungry as I am," thought Alec. He dropped down and drank from the spring.

Darkness came rapidly. Suddenly Alec felt the stillness of the island — no birds, no animals, no sounds. It was as if he and the Black were the only living creatures in the world. Millions of stars shone overhead and seemed so close. The moon rose high and round; its reflection cast upon the pool.

The Black looked up from his grazing. He, too, seemed to watch the moon. Alec whistled — low, then louder and fading. A moment of silence. Then the stallion's shrill whistle pierced the night. Alec saw the Black look in his direction and then continue searching for grass. He smiled and crawled into his shelter. The day's work had made him tired and he was soon asleep.

The next morning found Alec beside the cove again with his spear, determined to catch a fish for breakfast. At noon he ate berries. Mid-afternoon he was sick; his head whirled and he could hardly keep his eyes from closing.

A small whirlpool appeared on the surface of the water. Alec grabbed the spear beside him and rose to his knees. He saw a gray shape in the water below. He raised his spear and moved it along with the fish.

Then he plunged it! The spear quivered in its flight. He had hit! He jumped into the water, shoving the spear and fish against the bottom. He mustn't lose this one! His hand reached the knife. The fish was there wriggling, fighting. Then he had it. Quickly he raised the fish from the water and threw it, and the spear, onto the bank. Wearily he climbed up and looked at his catch. "Two feet if it's an inch," he said hungrily. He drew out the spear, picked up the fish and went back to camp.

Alec washed the fish in the spring. Then he placed it upon a piece of wood and scaled it. Now if he could only get a fire started. He remembered watching a man in India build a fire without matches. Perhaps he could do the same.

He gathered some small pieces of bark, dry wood and a deserted bird's nest, and spread them on the ground in front of him. He picked out the driest piece of wood and, with his knife, bored a hole halfway through it. Carefully he tore small threads of straw from the bird's nest and placed them inside the hole; they would ignite quickly. Next he cut a sturdy elastic branch about eighteen inches long from a nearby tree, skinned it and placed one end in the hole. He leaned on the stick, bending it, and then rapidly turned the curved part like a carpenter's bit.

It seemed to Alec that an hour passed before a small column of smoke crept out of the hole. His tired arms pushed harder. Slowly a small flame grew and then the dry wood was on fire. He added more wood. Then he snatched the fish, wrapped it in some seaweed which he had previously washed, and placed it on top of the fire.

Later, Alec removed the fish. He tried a piece and found it to be good. Famished, he tore into the rest of it.

The days passed and the boy strove desperately to find food to keep himself alive; he caught only one more fish — it would be impossible for him to depend upon the sea for his living. He turned again to the berries, but they were fast diminishing. He managed to keep his fire going as the heat made dry fuel plentiful. However, that was of little use to him as he had nothing to cook.

One day as Alec walked along the beach, he saw a large red shell in the distance. He gripped his spear tighter; it looked like a turtle. Then hunger made him lose all caution and he rushed forward, his spear raised. He threw himself upon the shell, his knife digging into the opening where he believed the turtle's head to be. Desperately he turned the huge shell over — it was empty, cleaned out; only the hollow shell met Alec's famished gaze. He stood still, dazed. Then slowly he turned and walked back to camp.

The Black was drinking from the spring. His large body too was beginning to show signs of starvation. Alec no longer felt any fear of him. The stallion raised his proud head and looked at the boy. Then he turned and trotted off. His mane, long and flowing, whipped in the wind. His whistle filled the air.

Alec watched him, envying his proud, wild spirit. The horse was used to the hardships of the desert; probably he would outlive him. The boy's subconscious thought rose to the surface of his mind: "There's food, Alec, food — if you could only find some way of killing him!" Then he shook his head, hating himself. Kill the animal that had saved his life? Never — even if he could, he would die of starvation first! The stallion reached the top of the hill and stood there, like a beautiful black statue, his gaze upon the open sea.

One morning Alec made his way weakly toward the rocky side of the island. He came to the huge rocks and climbed on top of one of them. It was more barren than any other part of the island. It was low tide and Alec's eyes wandered over the stony shore, looking for any kind of shellfish he might be able to eat. He noticed the mosslike substance on all the rocks at the water's edge, and on those that extended out. What was that stuff the biology teacher had made them eat last term in one of their experiments? Hadn't he called it *carragheen*? Yes, that was it. A sort of seaweed, he had said, that grew abundantly along the rocky parts of the Atlantic coast of Europe and North America. When washed and dried, it was edible for humans and livestock. Could the moss on the rocks below be it? Alec scarcely dared to hope.

Slowly Alec made the dangerous descent. He reached the water level and scrambled across the rocks. He took a handful of the soft greenish-yellow moss which covered them and raised it to his lips. It smelled the same. He tasted it. The moss was terribly salty from the sea, but it was the same as he had eaten that day in the classroom!

Eagerly he filled his pockets with it, then removed his shirt and filled it full. He climbed up again and hurried back to camp. There he emptied the moss onto the ground beside the spring. The next quarter of an hour he spent washing it, and then placed it out in the sun to dry. Hungrily he tasted it again. It was better — and it was food!

When he had finished eating, the sun was falling into the ocean, and the skies were rapidly growing dark. In the distance Alec saw the stallion coming toward the spring. Quickly he picked up some of the moss for himself and left the rest on the ground beside the pool. Would the Black eat it? Alec hurried to his shelter and stood still watching intently.

The stallion rushed up, shook his long neck and buried his mouth into the water. He drank long. When he had finished he looked toward the boy, then his pink nostrils quivered. The Black put his nose to the ground and walked toward the moss which Alec had left. He sniffed at it. Then he picked a little up and started eating. He chewed long and carefully. He reached down for more.

That night Alec slept better than he had since he had been on the island. He had found food — food to sustain him and the Black!

ZEBRA QUESTION

I ASKED the zebra,
Are you black with white stripes?
Or white with black stripes?
And the zebra asked me,
Are you good with bad habits?
Or are you bad with good habits?
Are you noisy with quiet times?
Or are you quiet with noisy times?
Are you happy with some sad days?
Or are you sad with some happy days?
Are you neat with some sloppy ways?
Or are you sloppy with some neat ways?
And on and on and on and on
And on and on he went.
I'll never ask a zebra
About stripes
Again.

FANTASTIC WORLDS

THE HUCKABUCK FAMILY...

... and how they raised popcorn in Nebraska and
quit and came back

ONAS Jonas Huckabuck was a farmer in Nebraska with a wife, Mama Mama Huckabuck, and a daughter, Pony Pony Huckabuck.

"Your father gave you two names the same in front," people had said to him.

And he answered, "Yes, two names are easier to remember. If you call me by my first name Jonas and I don't hear you, then when you call me by my second name Jonas, maybe I will.

"And," he went on, "I call my pony-face girl Pony Pony because if she doesn't hear me the first time, she always does the second."

And so they lived on a farm where they raised popcorn, these three, Jonas Jonas Huckabuck, his wife Mama Mama Huckabuck, and their pony-face daughter Pony Pony Huckabuck.

After they harvested the crop one year, they had the barns, the cribs, the sheds, the shacks, and all the cracks and corners of the farm, all filled with popcorn.

"We came out to Nebraska to raise popcorn," said Jonas Jonas, "and I guess we got nearly enough popcorn this year for the popcorn poppers and all the friends and relations of all the popcorn poppers in these United States."

And this was the year Pony Pony was going to bake her first squash pie all by herself. In one corner of the corncrib, all covered over with

popcorn, she had a secret, a big round squash, a fat yellow squash, a rich squash all spotted with spots of gold.

She carried the squash into the kitchen, took a long, sharp, shining knife, and then she cut the squash in the middle till she had two big half squashes. And inside just like outside, it was rich yellow spotted with spots of gold.

And there was a shine of silver. And Pony Pony wondered why silver should be in a squash. She picked and plunged with her fingers till she pulled it out.

"It's a buckle," she said, "a silver buckle, a Chinese silver slipper buckle."

She ran with it to her father and said, "Look what I found when I cut open the golden yellow squash spotted with gold spots — it is a Chinese silver slipper buckle."

"It means our luck is going to change, and we don't know whether it will be good luck or bad luck," said Jonas Jonas to his daughter, Pony Pony Huckabuck.

Then she ran with it to her mother and said, "Look what I found when I cut open the yellow squash spotted with spots of gold — it is a Chinese silver slipper buckle."

"It means our luck is going to change, and we don't know whether it will be good luck or bad luck," said Mama Mama Huckabuck.

And that night a fire started in the barns, crib, sheds, shacks, cracks, and corners, where the popcorn harvest was kept. All night long the popcorn popped. In the morning the ground all around the farmhouse and the barn was covered with white popcorn so it looked like a heavy fall of snow.

All the next day the fire kept on, and the popcorn popped till it was up to the shoulders of Pony Pony when she tried to walk from the house to the barn. And that night in all the barns, cribs, sheds, shacks, cracks, and corners of the farm, the popcorn went on popping.

In the morning when Jonas Jonas Huckabuck looked out of the upstairs window, he saw the popcorn popping and coming higher and higher. It was nearly up to the window. Before evening and dark of that day, Jonas Jonas Huckabuck, and his wife Mama Mama Huckabuck, and their daughter Pony Pony Huckabuck, all went away from the farm saying, "We came to Nebraska to raise popcorn, but this is too much. We will not come back till the wind blows away the popcorn. We will not come back till we get a sign and a signal."

They went to Oskaloosa, Iowa. And the next year Pony Pony Huckabuck was very proud because when she stood on the sidewalks in the street, she could see her father sitting high on the seat of a coal wagon, driving two big spanking horses hitched with shining brass harness in front of the coal wagon. And though Pony Pony and Jonas Jonas were proud, very proud all that year, there never came a sign, a signal.

The next year again was a proud year, exactly as proud a year as they spent in Oskaloosa. They went to Paducah, Kentucky, to Defiance, Ohio; Peoria, Illinois; Indianapolis, Indiana; Walla Walla, Washington. And in all these places Pony Pony Huckabuck saw her father, Jonas Jonas Huckabuck, standing in rubber boots deep down in a ditch with a shining steel shovel shoveling yellow clay and black mud from down in the ditch high and high up over his shoulders. And though it was a proud year, they got no sign, no signal.

The next year came. It was the proudest of all. This was the year Jonas Jonas Huckabuck and his family lived in Elgin, Illinois, and Jonas Jonas was watchman in a watch factory watching the watches.

"I know where you have been," Mama Mama Huckabuck would say of an evening to Pony Pony Huckabuck. "You have been down to the watch factory watching your father watch the watches."

"Yes," said Pony Pony. "Yes, and this evening when I was watching Father watch the watches in the watch factory, I looked over my left shoulder and I saw a policeman with a star and brass buttons, and he was watching me to see if I was watching Father watch the watches in the watch factory."

It was a proud year. Pony Pony saved her money. Thanksgiving came. Pony Pony said, "I am going to get a squash to make a squash pie." She hunted from one grocery to another; she kept her eyes on the farm wagons coming into Elgin with squashes.

She found what she wanted, the yellow squash spotted with gold spots. She took it home, cut it open, and saw the inside was like the outside, all rich yellow spotted with gold spots.

There was a shine like silver. She picked and plunged with her fingers and pulled and pulled till at last she pulled out the shine of silver.

"It's a sign; it is a signal," she said. "It is a buckle, a slipper buckle, a Chinese silver slipper buckle. It is the mate to the other buckle. Our luck is going to change. Yoo hoo! Yoo hoo!"

She told her father and mother about the buckle. They went back to the farm in Nebraska. The wind by this time had been blowing and blowing for three years, and all the popcorn was blown away.

"Now we are going to be farmers again," said Jonas Jonas Huckabuck to Mama Mama Huckabuck and to Pony Pony Huckabuck. "And we are going to raise cabbages, beets, and turnips; we are going to raise squash, rutabaga, pumpkins, and peppers for pickling. We are going to raise wheat, oats, barley, rye. We are going to raise corn such as Indian corn and kaffir corn — but we are *not* going to raise any popcorn for the popcorn poppers to be popping."

And the pony-face daughter, Pony Pony Huckabuck, was proud because she had on new black slippers, and around her ankles, holding the slippers on the left foot and the right foot, she had two buckles, silver buckles, Chinese silver slipper buckles. They were mates.

Sometimes on Thanksgiving Day and Christmas and New Year's she tells her friends to be careful when they open a squash.

"Squashes make your luck change good to bad and bad to good," says Pony Pony.

O G D E N   N A S H

THE TALE OF CUSTARD
THE DRAGON

ELINDA lived in a little white house,
With a little black kitten and a little gray mouse,
And a little yellow dog and a little red wagon,
And a realio, trulio, little pet dragon.

Now the name of the little black kitten was Ink,
And the little gray mouse, she called her Blink,
And the little yellow dog was sharp as Mustard,
But the dragon was a coward, and she called him Custard.

Custard the dragon had big sharp teeth,
And spikes on top of him and scales underneath,
Mouth like a fireplace, chimney for a nose,
And realio, trulio daggers on his toes.

Belinda was as brave as a barrel-full of bears,
And Ink and Blink chased lions down the stairs,
Mustard was as brave as a tiger in a rage,
But Custard cried for a nice safe cage.

Belinda tickled him, she tickled him unmerciful,
Ink, Blink and Mustard, they rudely called him Percival,
They all sat laughing in the little red wagon
At the realio, trulio, cowardly dragon.

Belinda giggled till she shook the house,
And Blink said *Weeek!*, which is giggling for a mouse,
Ink and Mustard rudely asked his age,
When Custard cried for a nice safe cage.

Suddenly, suddenly they heard a nasty sound,
And Mustard growled, and they all looked around.
Meowch! cried Ink, and Ooh! cried Belinda,
For there was a pirate, climbing in the winda.

Pistol in his left hand, pistol in his right,
And he held in his teeth a cutlass bright;
His beard was black, one leg was wood.
It was clear that the pirate meant no good.

Belinda paled, and she cried Help! Help!
But Mustard fled with a terrified yelp,
Ink trickled down to the bottom of the household,
And little mouse Blink strategically mouseholed.

But up jumped Custard, snorting like an engine,
Clashed his tail like irons in a dungeon,
With a clatter and a clank and a jangling squirm
He went at the pirate like a robin at a worm.

The pirate gaped at Belinda's dragon,
And gulped some grog from his pocket flagon,
He fired two bullets, but they didn't hit,
And Custard gobbled him, every bit.

Belinda embraced him, Mustard licked him;
No one mourned for his pirate victim.
Ink and Blink in glee did gyrate
Around the dragon that ate the pyrate.

Belinda still lives in her little white house,
With her little black kitten and her little gray mouse,
And her little yellow dog and her little red wagon,
And her realio, trulio, little pet dragon.

Belinda is as brave as a barrel-full of bears,
And Ink and Blink chase lions down the stairs,
Mustard is as brave as a tiger in rage,
But Custard keeps crying for a nice safe cage.

THE SCARECROW AND THE TIN WOODMAN

HERE lived in the Land of Oz two queerly made men who were the best of friends. They were so much happier when together that they were seldom apart; yet they liked to separate, once in a while, that they might enjoy the pleasure of meeting again.

One was a Scarecrow. That means he was a suit of blue Munchkin clothes, stuffed with straw, on top of which was fastened a round cloth head, filled with bran to hold it in shape. On the head were painted two eyes, two ears, a nose and a mouth. The Scarecrow had never been much of a success in scaring crows, but he prided himself on being a superior man, because he could feel no pain, was never tired, and did not have to eat or drink. His brains were sharp, for the Wizard of Oz had put pins and needles in the Scarecrow's brains.

The other man was made all of tin, his arms and legs and head being cleverly jointed so that he could move them freely. He was known as the Tin Woodman, having at one time been a woodchopper, and everyone loved him because the Wizard had given him an excellent heart of red plush.

The Tin Woodman lived in a magnificent tin castle, built on his country estate in the Winkie Land, not far from the Emerald City of Oz. It had pretty tin furniture and was surrounded by lovely gardens in

which were many tin trees and beds of tin flowers. The palace of the Scarecrow was not far distant, on the banks of a river, and this palace was in the shape of an immense ear of corn.

One morning the Tin Woodman went to visit his friend the Scarecrow, and as they had nothing better to do they decided to take a boat ride on the river. So they got into the Scarecrow's boat, which was formed from a big corncob, hollowed out and pointed at both ends and decorated around the edges with brilliant jewels. The sail was of purple silk and glittered gayly in the sunshine.

There was a good breeze that day, so the boat glided swiftly over the water. By and by they came to a smaller river that flowed out from a deep forest, and the Tin Woodman proposed they sail up this stream, as it would be cool and shady beneath the trees of the forest. So the Scarecrow, who was steering, turned the boat up the stream and the friends continued talking together of old times and the wonderful adventures they had met with while traveling with Dorothy, the little Kansas girl. They became so much interested in this talk that they forgot to notice that the boat was now sailing through the forest, or that the stream was growing more narrow and crooked.

Suddenly the Scarecrow glanced up and saw a big rock just ahead of them.

"Look out!" he cried; but the warning came too late.

The Tin Woodman sprang to his feet just as the boat bumped into the rock, and the jar made him lose his balance. He toppled and fell overboard and being made of tin he sank to the bottom of the water in an instant and lay there at full length, face up.

Immediately the Scarecrow threw out the anchor, so as to hold the boat in that place, and then he leaned over the side and through the clear water looked at his friend sorrowfully.

"Dear me!" he exclaimed; "what a misfortune."

"It is, indeed," replied the Tin Woodman, speaking in muffled tones because so much water covered him. "I cannot drown, of course, but I must lie here until you find a way to get me out. Meantime, the

water is soaking into all my joints and I shall become badly rusted before I am rescued."

"Very true," agreed the Scarecrow; "but be patient, my friend, and I'll dive down and get you. My straw will not rust, and is easily replaced, if damaged, so I'm not afraid of the water."

The Scarecrow now took off his hat and made a dive from the boat into the water; but he was so light in weight that he barely dented the surface of the stream, nor could he reach the Tin Woodman with his outstretched straw arms. So he floated to the boat and climbed into it, saying the while:

"Do not despair, my friend. We have an extra anchor aboard, and I will tie it around my waist, to make me sink, and dive again."

"Don't do that!" called the tin man. "That would anchor you also to the bottom, where I am, and we'd both be helpless."

"True enough," sighed the Scarecrow, wiping his wet face with a handkerchief; and then he gave a cry of astonishment, for he found he had wiped off one painted eye and now had but one eye to see with.

"How dreadful!" said the poor Scarecrow. "That eye must have been painted in watercolor, instead of oil. I must be careful not to wipe off the other eye, for then I could not see to help you at all."

A shriek of elfish laughter greeted this speech and looking up the Scarecrow found the trees full of black crows, who seemed much amused by the straw man's one-eyed countenance. He knew the crows well, however, and they had usually been friendly to him because he had never deceived them into thinking he was a meat man — the sort of man they really feared.

"Don't laugh," said he; "you may lose an eye yourselves, some day."

"We couldn't look as funny as you, if we did," replied one old crow, the king of them. "But what has gone wrong with you?"

"The Tin Woodman, my dear friend and companion, has fallen overboard and is now on the bottom of the river," said the Scarecrow. "I'm trying to get him out again, but I fear I shall not succeed."

"Why, it's easy enough," declared the old crow. "Tie a string to him and all of my crows will fly down, take hold of the string, and pull him up out of the water. There are hundreds of us here, so our united strength could lift much more than that."

"But I can't tie a string to him," replied the Scarecrow. "My straw is so light that I am unable to dive through the water. I've tried it, and knocked one eye out."

"Can't you fish for him?"

"Ah, that is a good idea," said the Scarecrow. "I'll make the attempt."

He found a fishline in the boat, with a stout hook at the end of it. No bait was needed, so the Scarecrow dropped the hook into the water till it touched the Woodman.

"Hook it into a joint," advised the crow, who was now perched upon a branch that stuck far out and bent down over the water.

The Scarecrow tried to do this, but having only one eye he could not see the joints very clearly.

"Hurry up, please," begged the Tin Woodman; "you've no idea how damp it is down here."

"Can't you help?" asked the crow.

"How?" inquired the tin man.

"Catch the line and hook it around your neck."

The Tin Woodman made the attempt and after several trials wound the line around his neck and hooked it securely.

"Good!" cried the King Crow, a mischievous old fellow. "Now, then, we'll all grab the line and pull you out."

At once the air was filled with black crows, each of whom seized the cord with beak or talons. The Scarecrow watched them with much interest and forgot that he had tied the other end of the line around his own waist, so he would not lose it while fishing for his friend.

"All together for the good caws!" shrieked the King Crow, and with a great flapping of wings the birds rose into the air.

The Scarecrow clapped his stuffed hands in glee as he saw his friend drawn from the water into the air; but next moment the straw man was himself in the air, his stuffed legs kicking wildly; for the crows had flown straight up through the trees. On one end of the line dangled the Tin Woodman, hung by the neck, and on the other dangled the Scarecrow, hung by the waist and clinging fast to the spare anchor of the boat, which he had seized hoping to save himself.

"Hi, there — be careful!" shouted the Scarecrow to the crows. "Don't take us so high. Land us on the river bank."

But the crows were bent on mischief. They thought it a good joke to bother the two, now that they held them captive.

"Here's where the crows scare the Scarecrow!" chuckled the naughty King Crow, and at his command the birds flew over the forest to where a tall dead tree stood higher than all the other trees. At the very top was a crotch, formed by two dead limbs, and into the crotch the crows dropped the center of the line. Then, letting go their hold, they flew away, chattering with laughter, and left the two friends suspended high in the air — one on each side of the tree.

Now the Tin Woodman was much heavier than the Scarecrow, but the reason they balanced so nicely was because the straw man still clung fast to the iron anchor. There they hung, not ten feet apart, yet unable to reach the bare tree-trunk.

"For goodness' sake don't drop that anchor," said the Tin Wood-man anxiously.

"Why not?" inquired the Scarecrow.

"If you did I'd tumble to the ground, where my tin would be badly dented by the fall. Also you would shoot into the air and alight somewhere among the tree-tops."

"Then," said the Scarecrow, earnestly, "I shall hold fast to the anchor."

For a time they both dangled in silence, the breeze swaying them gently to and fro. Finally the tin man said: "Here is an emergency, friend, where only brains can help us. We must think of some way to escape."

"I'll do the thinking," replied the Scarecrow. "My brains are the sharpest."

He thought so long that the tin man grew tired and tried to change his position, but found his joints had already rusted so badly that he could not move them. And his oil-can was back in the boat.

"Do you suppose your brains are rusted, friend Scarecrow?" he asked in a weak voice, for his jaws would scarcely move.

"No, indeed. Ah, here's an idea at last!"

With this the Scarecrow clapped his hands to his head, forgetting the anchor, which tumbled to the ground. The result was astonishing; for, just as the tin man had said, the light Scarecrow flew into the air, sailed over the top of the tree and landed in a bramble-bush, while the tin man fell plump to the ground, and landing on a bed of dry leaves was not dented at all. The Tin Woodman's joints were so rusted, however, that he was unable to move, while the thorns held the Scarecrow a fast prisoner.

While they were in this sad plight the sound of hoofs was heard and along the forest path rode the little Wizard of Oz, seated on a wooden Sawhorse. He smiled when he saw the one-eyed head of the Scarecrow sticking out of the bramble-bush, but he helped the poor straw man out of his prison.

"Thank you, dear Wiz," said the grateful Scarecrow. "Now we must get the oil-can and rescue the Tin Woodman."

Together they ran to the river bank, but the boat was floating in midstream and the Wizard was obliged to mumble some magic words to draw it to the bank, so the Scarecrow could get the oil-can. Then back they flew to the tin man, and while the Scarecrow carefully oiled each joint the little Wizard moved the joints gently back and forth until they worked freely. After an hour of this labor the Tin Woodman was again on his feet, and although still a little stiff he managed to walk to the boat.

The Wizard and the Sawhorse also got aboard the corncob craft and together they returned to the Scarecrow's palace. But the Tin Woodman was very careful not to stand up in the boat again.

JACK PRELUTSKY

AN IRRITATING CREATURE

THERE'S an irritating creature
in my living room today,
it's been here for a year now,
and it will not go away.
The first time that I saw it,
it was in my easy chair,
and displayed no inclination
to forsake its station there.

I put it in a parcel,
and I left it at the store,
the thing was there to greet me
when I opened up my door,
I took it to the forest,
and I tied it to a tree,
I found it in my kitchen
having sandwiches and tea.

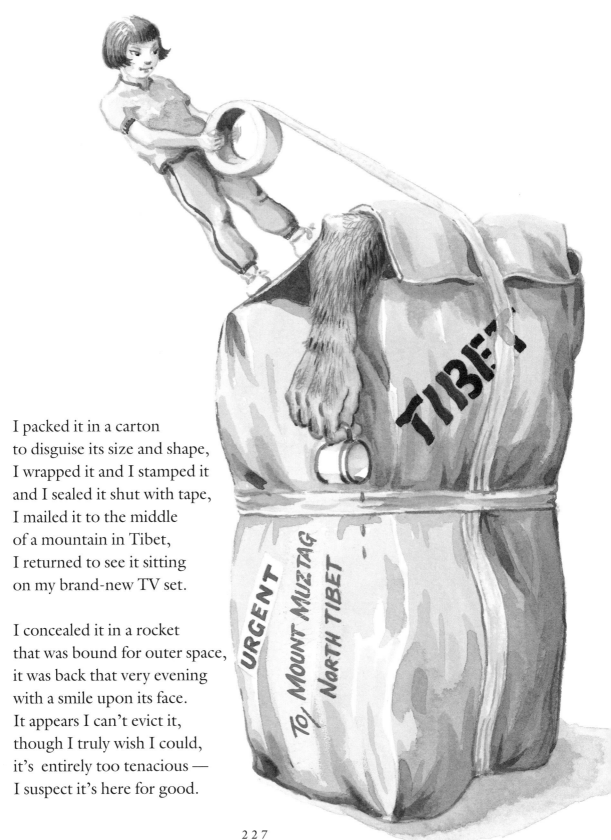

I packed it in a carton
to disguise its size and shape,
I wrapped it and I stamped it
and I sealed it shut with tape,
I mailed it to the middle
of a mountain in Tibet,
I returned to see it sitting
on my brand-new TV set.

I concealed it in a rocket
that was bound for outer space,
it was back that very evening
with a smile upon its face.
It appears I can't evict it,
though I truly wish I could,
it's entirely too tenacious —
I suspect it's here for good.

JANE YOLEN

THE POT CHILD

HERE was once an ill-humored potter who lived all alone and made his way by shaping clay into cups and bowls and urns. His pots were colored with the tones of the earth, and on their sides he painted all creatures excepting man.

"For there was never a human I liked well enough to share my house and my life with," said the bitter old man.

But one day, when the potter was known throughout the land for his sharp tongue as well as his pots, and so old that even death might have come as a friend, he sat down and on the side of a large bisque urn he drew a child.

The child was without flaw in the outline, and so the potter colored in its form with earth glazes; rutile for the body and cobalt blue for the eyes. And to the potter's practiced eye, the figure on the pot was perfect.

So he put the pot into the kiln, closed up the door with bricks, and set the flame.

Slowly the fires burned. And within the kiln the glazes matured and turned their proper tones.

It was a full day and a night before the firing was done. And a full day and a night before the kiln had cooled. And it was a full day and a night before the old potter dared unbrick the kiln door. For the pot child was his masterpiece, of this he was sure.

At last, though, he could put it off no longer. He took down the kiln door, reached in, and removed the urn.

Slowly he felt along the pot's side. It was smooth and still warm. He set the pot on the ground and walked around it, nodding his head as he went.

The child on the pot was so lifelike, it seemed to follow him with its lapis eyes. Its skin was a pearly yellow-white, and each hair on its head like beaten gold.

So the old potter squatted down before the urn, examining the figure closely, checking it for cracks and flaws. But there were none. He drew in his breath at the child's beauty and thought to himself. "*There is one I might like well enough.*" And when he expelled his breath again, he blew directly on the image's lips.

At that, the pot child sighed and stepped off the urn.

Well, this so startled the old man that he fell back into the dust.

After a while, though, the potter saw that the pot child was waiting for him to speak. So he stood up and in a brusque tone said "Well, then, come here. Let me look at you."

The child ran over to him and, ignoring his tone, put its arms around his waist, and whispered "Father" in a high sweet voice.

This so startled the old man that he was speechless for the first time in his life. And as he could not find the words to tell the child to go, it stayed. Yet after a day, when he had found the words, the potter knew he could not utter them for the child's perfect face and figure had enchanted him.

When the potter worked or ate or slept, the child was by his side, speaking when spoken to but otherwise still. It was a pot child, after all, and not a real child. It did not join him in his work but was content to watch. When other people came to the old man's shop, the child stepped back onto the urn and did not move. Only the potter knew it was alive.

One day several famous people came to the potter's shop. He showed them all around, grudgingly, touching one pot and then another. He answered their questions in a voice that was crusty and hard. But they knew his reputation and did not answer back.

At last they came to the urn.

The old man stood before it and sighed. It was such an uncharacteristic sound that the people looked at him strangely. But the potter did not notice. He simply stood for a moment more, then said, "This is the Pot Child. It is my masterpiece. I shall never make another one so fine."

He moved away, and one woman said after him. "It *is* good." But turning to her companions, she added in a low voice. "But it is *too* perfect for me."

A man with her agreed. "It lacks something," he whispered back.

The woman thought a moment. "It has no heart," she said. "That is what is wrong."

"It has no soul," he amended.

They nodded at each other and turned away from the urn. The woman picked out several small bowls, and, paying for them, she and the others went away.

No sooner were the people out of sight than the pot child stepped down from the urn.

"Father," the pot child asked, "what is a heart?"

"A vastly overrated part of the body," said the old man gruffly. He turned to work the clay on his wheel.

"Then," thought the pot child, "I am better off without one." It watched as the clay grew first tall and then wide between the potter's knowing palms. It hesitated asking another question, but at last could bear it no longer.

"And what is a soul, Father?" asked the pot child. "Why did you not draw one on me when you made me on the urn?"

The potter looked up in surprise. "Draw one? No one can draw a soul."

The child's disappointment was so profound, the potter added, "A man's body is like a pot, which does not disclose what is inside. Only when the pot is poured, do we see its contents. Only when a man acts, do we know what kind of soul he has."

The pot child seemed happy with that explanation, and the potter went back to his work. But over the next few weeks the child continually got in his way. When the potter worked the clay, the pot child tried to bring him water to keep the clay moist. But it spilled the water and the potter pushed the child away.

When the potter carried the unfired pots to the kiln, the pot child tried to carry some, too. But it dropped the pots, and many were shattered. The potter started to cry out in anger, bit his tongue, and was still.

When the potter went to fire the kiln, the pot child tried to light the flame. Instead, it blew out the fire.

At last the potter cried, "You heartless thing. Leave me to do my work. It is all I have. How am I to keep body and soul together when I am so plagued by you?"

At these words, the pot child sat down in the dirt, covered its face, and wept. Its tiny body heaved so with its sobs that the potter feared it would break in two. His crusty old heart softened, and he went over to the child and said, "There, child. I did not mean to shout so. What is it that ails you?"

The pot child looked up. "Oh, my Father, I know I have no heart.

But that is a vastly overrated part of the body. Still, I was trying to show how I was growing a soul."

The old man looked startled for a minute, but then, recalling their conversation of many weeks before, he said "My poor pot child, no one can *grow* a soul. It is there from birth." He touched the child lightly on the head.

The potter had meant to console the child, but at that the child cried even harder than before. Drops sprang from its eyes and ran down its cheeks like blue glaze. "Then I shall never have a soul," the pot child cried. "For I was not born but made."

Seeing how the child suffered, the old man took a deep breath. And when he let it out again, he said, "Child, as I made you, now I will make you a promise. When I die, you shall have *my* soul for then I shall no longer need it."

"Oh, then I will be truly happy," said the pot child, slipping its little hand gratefully into the old man's. It did not see the look of pain that crossed the old man's face. But when it looked up at him and smiled, the old man could not help but smile back.

That very night, under the watchful eyes of the pot child, the potter wrote out his will. It was a simple paper, but it took a long time to compose for words did not come easily to the old man. Yet as he wrote, he felt surprisingly lightened. And the pot child smiled at him all the while. At last, after many scratchings out, it was done. The potter read the paper aloud to the pot child.

"It is good," said the pot child. "You do not suppose I will have long to wait for my soul?"

The old man laughed. "Not long, child."

And then the old man slept, tired after the late night's labor. But he had been so busy writing, he had forgotten to bank his fire, and in the darkest part of the night, the flames went out.

In the morning the shop was ice cold, and so was the old man. He did not waken, and without him, the pot child could not move from its shelf.

Later in the day, when the first customers arrived, they found the old man. And beneath his cold fingers lay a piece of paper that said:

> When I am dead, place my body in
> my kiln and light the flames. And
> when I am nothing but ashes, let
> those ashes be placed inside the
> Pot Child. For I would be one, body
> and soul, with the earth I have worked.

So it was done as the potter wished. And when the kiln was opened up, the people of the town placed the ashes in the ice-cold urn.

At the touch of the hot ashes, the pot cracked: once across the breast of the child and two small fissures under its eyes.

"What a shame," said the people to one another on seeing that. "We should have waited until the ashes cooled."

Yet the pot was still so beautiful, and the old potter so well known, that the urn was placed at once in a museum. Many people came to gaze on it.

One of those was the woman who had seen the pot that day so long ago at the shop.

"Why, look," she said to her companions. "It is the pot the old man called his masterpiece. It *is* good. But I like it even better now with those small cracks."

"Yes," said one of her companions, "it was too perfect before."

"Now the pot child has real character," said the woman. "It has . . . heart."

"Yes," added the same companion, "it has soul."

And they spoke so loudly that all the people around them heard. The story of their conversation was printed and repeated throughout the land, and everyone who went by the pot stopped and murmured, as if part of a ritual, "Look at that pot child. It has such heart. It has such soul."

ARNA BONTEMPS

LONESOME BOY

WHEN Bubber first learned to play the trumpet, his old grandpa winked his eye and laughed.

"You better mind how you blow that horn, sonny boy. You better mind."

"I like to blow loud, I like to blow fast, and I like to blow high," Bubber answered. "Listen to this, Grandpa." And he went on blowing with his eyes closed.

When Bubber was a little bigger, he began carrying his trumpet around with him wherever he went, so his old grandpa scratched his whiskers, took the corncob pipe out of his mouth, and laughed again.

"You better mind *where* you blow that horn, boy," he warned. "I used to blow one myself, and I know."

Bubber smiled. "Where did you ever blow music, Grandpa?"

"Down in New Orleans and all up and down the river. I blowed trumpet most everywhere in my young days, and I tell you, you better mind where you go blowing."

"I like to blow my trumpet in the school band when it marches, I like to blow it on the landing when the river boats come in sight, and I like to blow it among the trees in the swamp," he said, still smiling. But when he looked at his grandpa again, he saw a worried look on the

old man's face, and he asked, "What's the matter, Grandpa, ain't that all right?"

Grandpa shook his head. "I wouldn't do it if I was you."

That sounded funny to Bubber, but he was not in the habit of disputing his grandfather. Instead he said, "I don't believe I ever heard you blow the trumpet, Grandpa. Don't you want to try blowing on mine now?"

Again the old man shook his head. "My blowing days are long gone," he said. "I still got the lip, but I ain't got the teeth. It takes good teeth to blow high notes on a horn, and these I got ain't much good. They're store teeth."

That made Bubber feel sorry for his grandfather, so he whispered softly, "I'll mind where I blow my horn, Grandpa."

He didn't really mean it though. He just said it to make his grandpa feel good. And the very next day he was half a mile out in the country blowing his horn in a cornfield. Two or three evenings later he was blowing it on a shady lane when the sun went down and not paying much attention where he went.

When he came home, his grandpa met him. "I heard you blowing your horn a long ways away," he said. "The air was still. I could hear it easy."

"How did it sound, Grandpa?"

"Oh, it sounded right pretty." He paused a moment, knocking the ashes out of his pipe, before adding, "Sounded like you mighta been lost."

That made Bubber ashamed of himself, because he knew he had not kept his word and that he was not minding where he blew his trumpet. "I know what you mean, Grandpa," he answered. "But I can't do like you say. When I'm blowing my horn, I don't always look where I'm going."

Grandpa walked to the window and looked out. While he was standing there, he hitched his overalls up a little higher. He took a red handkerchief from his pocket and wiped his forehead. "Sounded to me like you might have been past Barbin's Landing."

"I was lost," Bubber admitted.

"You can end up in some funny places when you're just blowing a horn and not paying attention. I know," Grandpa insisted. "I know."

"Well, what do you want me to do, Grandpa?"

The old man struck a kitchen match on the seat of his pants and lit a kerosene lamp, because the room was black dark by now. While the match was still burning, he lit his pipe. Then he sat down and stretched out his feet. Bubber was on a stool on the other side of the room, his trumpet under his arm. "When you go to school and play your horn in the band, that's all right," the old man said. "When you come home, you ought to put it in the case and leave it there. It ain't good to go traipsing around with a horn in your hand. You might get into devilment."

"But I feel lonesome without my trumpet, Grandpa," Bubber pleaded. "I don't like to go around without it any time. I feel lost."

Grandpa sighed. "Well, there you are — lost with it and lost without it. I don't know what's going to become of you, sonny boy."

"You don't understand, Grandpa. You don't understand."

The old man smoked his pipe quietly for a few minutes and then went off to bed, but Bubber did not move. Later on, however, when he heard his grandpa snoring in the next room, he went outdoors, down the path and around the smokehouse, and sat on a log. The night was still. He couldn't hear anything louder than a cricket. Soon he began wondering how his trumpet would sound on such a still night, back there behind the old smokehouse, so he put the mouthpiece to his lips very lightly and blew a few silvery notes. Immediately Bubber felt better. Now he knew for sure that Grandpa didn't understand how it was with a boy and a horn — a lonesome boy with a silver trumpet. Bubber lifted his horn toward the stars and let the music pour out.

Presently a big orange moon rose, and everything Bubber could see changed suddenly. The moon was so big it made the smokehouse and the trees and the fences seem small. Bubber blew his trumpet loud, he blew it fast, and he blew it high, and in just a few minutes he forgot all about Grandpa sleeping in the house.

He was afraid to talk to Grandpa after that. He was afraid Grandpa

might scold him or warn him or try in some other way to persuade him to leave his trumpet in its case. Bubber was growing fast now. He knew what he liked, and he did not think he needed any advice from Grandpa.

Still, he loved his grandfather very much, and he had no intention of saying anything that would hurt him. Instead he decided to leave home. He did not tell Grandpa what he was going to do. He just waited till the old man went to sleep in his bed one night. Then he quietly blew out the lamp, put his trumpet under his arm and started walking down the road from Marksville to Barbin's Landing.

No boat was there, but Bubber did not mind. He knew one would come before morning, and he knew that he would not be lonesome so long as he had his trumpet with him. He found a place on the little dock where he could lean back against a post and swing his feet over the edge while playing, and the time passed swiftly. And when he finally went aboard a river boat, just before morning, he found a place on the deck that suited him just as well and went right on blowing his horn.

Nobody asked him to pay any fare. The river boat men did not seem to expect it of a boy who blew a trumpet the way Bubber did. And in New Orleans the cooks in the kitchen where he ate and the people who kept the rooming houses where he slept did not seem to expect him to pay either. In fact, people seemed to think that a boy who played a trumpet where the patrons of a restaurant could hear him or for the guests of a rooming house should receive money for it. They began to throw money around Bubber's feet as he played his horn.

At first he was surprised. Later he decided it only showed how wrong Grandpa had been about horn blowing. So he picked up all the money they threw, bought himself fancy new clothes and began looking for new places to play. He ran into boys who played guitars or bullfiddles or drums or other instruments, and he played right along with them. He went out with them to play for picnics or barbecues or boat excursions or dances. He played early in the morning and he played late at night, and he bought new clothes and dressed up so fine he scarcely knew himself in a mirror. He scarcely knew day from night.

It was wonderful to play the trumpet like that, Bubber thought, and to make all that money. People telephoned to the rooming house where he lived and asked for him nearly every day. Some sent notes asking if he would play his trumpet at their parties. Occasionally one would send an automobile to bring him to the place. Bubber liked riding through the pretty part of the city to the ballrooms in which well-dressed people waited to dance to his music. He enjoyed even more the times when he was taken to big white-columned houses in the country, houses surrounded by old trees with moss on them.

But he went to so many places to play his trumpet, he forgot where he had been and he got into the habit of not paying much attention. That was how it was the day he received a strange call on the telephone. A voice that sounded like a very proper gentleman said, "I would like to speak to the boy from Marksville, the one who plays the trumpet."

"I'm Bubber, sir. I'm the one."

"Well, Bubber, I'm having a very special party tonight — very special," the voice said. "I want you to play for us."

Bubber felt a little drowsy because he had been sleeping when the phone rang, and he still wasn't too well awake. He yawned as he answered, "Just me, sir? You want me to play by myself?"

"There will be other musicians, Bubber. You'll play in the band. We'll be looking for you."

"Where do you live, sir?" Bubber asked sleepily.

"Never mind about that, Bubber, I'll send my chauffeur with my car. He'll bring you."

The voice was growing faint by this time, and Bubber was not sure he caught the last words. "Where did you say, sir?" he asked suddenly. "When is it you want me?"

"I'll send my chauffeur," the voice repeated and then faded out completely.

Bubber put the phone down and went back to his bed to sleep some more. He had played his trumpet very late the night before, and now he just couldn't keep his eyes open.

Something was ringing when he woke up again. Was it the telephone? Bubber jumped out of bed and ran to answer, but the phone buzzed when he put it to his ear. There was nobody on the line. Then he knew it must have been the doorbell. A moment later he heard the door open, and footsteps came down the dark hall toward his room. Before Bubber could turn on the light, the footsteps were just outside his room, and a man's voice said, "I'm the chauffeur. I've brought the car to take you to the dance."

"So soon?" Bubber asked, surprised.

The man laughed. "You must have slept all day. It's night now, and we have a long way to drive."

"I'll put on my clothes," Bubber said.

The street light was shining through the window, so he did not bother to switch on the light in his room. Bubber never liked to open his eyes with a bright light shining, and anyway he knew right where to put his hands on the clothes he needed. As he began slipping into them, the chauffeur turned away. "I'll wait for you on the curb," he said.

"All right," Bubber called. "I'll hurry."

When he finished dressing, Bubber took his trumpet off the shelf, closed the door of his room, and went out to where the tall chauffeur was standing beside a long, shiny automobile. The chauffeur saw him coming and opened the door to the back seat. When Bubber stepped in, he threw a lap robe across his knees and closed the door. Then the chauffeur went around to his place in the front seat, stepped on the starter, switched on his headlights, and sped away.

The car was finer than any Bubber had ridden in before, and the motor purred so softly, the chauffeur drove it so smoothly, Bubber soon

began to feel sleepy again. One thing puzzled him, however. He had not yet seen the chauffeur's face, and he wondered what the man looked like. But now the chauffeur's cap was down so far over his eyes and his coat collar was turned up so high Bubber could not see his face at all, no matter how far he leaned forward.

After a while he decided it was no use. He would have to wait till he got out of the car to look at the man's face. In the meantime he would sleep. Bubber pulled the lap robe up over his shoulders, stretched out on the wide back seat of the car and went to sleep again.

The car came to a stop, but Bubber did not wake up till the chauffeur opened the door and touched his shoulder. When he stepped out of the car, he could see nothing but dark, twisted trees with moss hanging from them. It was a dark and lonely place, and Bubber was so surprised he did not remember to look at the chauffeur's face. Instead, he followed the tall figure up a path covered with leaves to a white-columned house with lights shining in the windows.

Bubber felt a little better when he saw the big house with the bright windows. He had played in such houses before, and he was glad for a chance to play in another. He took his trumpet from under his arm, put the mouthpiece to his lips and blew a few bright, clear notes as he walked. The chauffeur did not turn around. He led Bubber to a side entrance, opened the door and pointed the boy to the room where the dancing had already started. Without ever showing his face, the chauffeur closed the door and returned to the car.

Nobody had to tell Bubber what to do now. He found a place next to the big fiddle that made the rhythms, waited a moment for the beat, then came in with his trumpet. With the bass fiddle, the drums, and the other stringed instruments backing him up, Bubber began to bear down on his trumpet. This was just what he liked. He played loud, he played fast, he played high, and it was all he could do to keep from laughing when he thought about Grandpa and remembered how the old man had told him to mind how he played his horn. Grandpa should see him now, Bubber thought.

Bubber looked at the dancers swirling on the ballroom floor under the high swinging chandelier, and he wished that Grandpa could somehow be at the window and see how they glided and spun around to the music of his horn. He wished the old man could get at least one glimpse of the handsome dancers, the beautiful women in bright-colored silks, the slender men in black evening clothes.

As the evening went on, more people came and began dancing. The floor became more and more crowded, and Bubber played louder and louder, faster and faster, and by midnight the gay ballroom seemed to be spinning like a pinwheel. The floor looked like glass under the dancers' feet. The draperies on the windows were like gold, and Bubber was playing his trumpet so hard and so fast his eyes looked ready to pop out of his head.

But he was not tired. He felt as if he could go on playing like this forever. He did not even need a short rest. When the other musicians called for a break and went outside to catch a breath of fresh air, he kept right on blowing his horn, running up the scale and down, hitting high C's, swelling out on the notes and then letting them fade away. He kept the dancers entertained till the full band came back, and he blew the notes that started them to dancing again.

Bubber gave no thought to the time, and when a breeze began blowing through the tall windows, he paid no attention. He played as loud as ever, and the dancers whirled just as fast. But there was one thing that did bother him a little. The faces of the dancers began to look thin and hollow as the breeze brought streaks of morning mist into the room. What was the matter with them? Were they tired from dancing all night? Bubber wondered.

But the morning breeze blew stronger and stronger. The curtains flapped, and a gray light appeared in the windows. By this time Bubber noticed that the people who were dancing had no faces at all, and though they continued to dance wildly as he played his trumpet, they seemed dim and far away. Were they disappearing?

Soon Bubber could scarcely see them at all. Suddenly he wondered where the party had gone. The musicians too grew dim and finally disappeared. Even the room with the big chandelier and the golden draperies at the windows was fading away like a dream. Bubber was frightened when he realized that nothing was left, and he was alone. Yes, definitely, he was alone, but — but *where*? Where was he now?

He never stopped blowing his shiny trumpet. In fact, as the party began to break up in this strange way, he blew harder than ever to help himself feel brave again. He also closed his eyes. That is how he happened to notice how uncomfortable the place where he was sitting had become. It was about as unpleasant as sitting on a log. And it was while his eyes were closed that he first became aware of leaves near by, leaves rustling and blowing in the cool breeze.

But he could not keep his eyes closed for long with so much happening. Bubber just had to peep eventually, and when he did, he saw only leaves around him. Certainly leaves were nothing to be afraid of, he thought, but it was a little hard to understand how the house and room in which he had been playing for the party all night had been replaced by branches and leaves like this. Bubber opened both his eyes wide, stopped blowing his horn for a moment and took a good, careful look at his surroundings.

Only then did he discover for sure that he was not in a house at all. There were no dancers, no musicians, nobody at all with him, and what had seemed like a rather uncomfortable chair or log was a large branch. Bubber was sitting in a pecan tree, and now he realized that this was where he had been blowing his trumpet so fast and so loud and so high all night. It was very discouraging.

But where was the chauffeur who had brought him here and what had become of the party and the graceful dancers? Bubber climbed down and began looking around. He could see no trace of the things that had seemed so real last night, so he decided he had better go home. Not home to the rooming house where he slept while in New Orleans, but home to the country where Grandpa lived.

He carried his horn under his arm, but he did not play a note on the bus that took him back to Marksville next day. And when he got off the bus and started walking down the road to Grandpa's house in the country, he still didn't feel much like playing anything on his trumpet.

Grandpa was sleeping in a hammock under a chinaberry tree when he arrived, but he slept with one eye open, so Bubber did not have to wake him up. He just stood there, and Grandpa smiled.

"I looked for you to come home before now," the old man said.

"I should have come sooner, Grandpa," Bubber answered, shamefaced.

"I expected you to be blowing on your horn when you came."

"That's what I want to talk to you about, Grandpa."

The old man sat up in the hammock and put his feet on the ground. He scratched his head and reached for his hat. "Don't tell me anything startling," he said. "I just woke up, and I don't want to be surprised so soon."

Bubber thought maybe he should not mention what had happened. "All right, Grandpa," he whispered, looking rather sad. He leaned against the chinaberry tree, holding the trumpet under his arm, and waited for Grandpa to speak again.

Suddenly the old man blinked his eyes as if remembering something he had almost forgotten. "Did you mind how you blew on that horn down in New Orleans?" he asked.

"Sometimes I did. Sometimes I *didn't*," Bubber confessed.

Grandpa looked hurt. "I hate to hear that, sonny boy," he said. "Have you been playing your horn at barbecues and boatrides and dances and all such as that?"

"Yes, Grandpa," Bubber said, looking at the ground.

"Keep on like that and you're apt to wind up playing for a devil's ball."

Bubber nodded sadly. "Yes, I know."

Suddenly the old man stood up and put his hand on Bubber's shoulder. "Did a educated gentleman call you on the telephone?"

"He talked so proper I could hardly make out what he was saying."

"Did the chauffeur come in a long shiny car?"

Bubber nodded again. "How did you know about all that, Grandpa?"

"Didn't I tell you I used to blow music, sonny boy?" Grandpa closed his eyes a moment. When he opened them again, he shook his head slowly. "Any time a boy with a trumpet takes off for New Orleans without telling anybody good-bye — well, sooner or later, one way or another, he's apt to hear from strange people."

"I should have hung up the telephone," Bubber mumbled, feeling ashamed of himself.

Suddenly Grandpa's voice grew stern. "You should have minded what I told you at the first. Blow your horn when you're a-mind to, but put it down when you're through. When you go traipsing through the woods, leave it on the shelf. When you feel lonesome, don't touch it. A horn can't do nothing for lonesomeness but make it hurt worse. When you're lonesome, that's the time to go out and find somebody to talk to. Come back to your trumpet when the house is full of company or when people's passing on the street. That's what I tried to tell you before."

"I'm going to mind you this time, Grandpa," Bubber promised. "I'm going to mind every word you say."

Grandpa laughed through his whiskers. "Well, take your trumpet in the house and put it on the shelf while I get you something to eat," he said. "Raising up a boy like you ain't easy. First you tell him when to pick up his horn, then you tell him when to put it down. Some things he just has to learn for himself, I reckon."

Bubber smiled too. He was hungry, and he had not tasted any of Grandpa's cooking for a long time.

SLIPPERS

YEARS ago in China, there was a poor couple who had no children. They prayed often, but they were in their fifties before Heaven heard them and sent them a little girl.

They loved her all the more because having a child had once seemed so impossible. They even called her their miracle child. But when she was still very small, her mother died, and she, despite her youth, took over the household.

"She'll kill herself with work," the other villagers scolded her father.

Her father threw up his hands in frustration. "I know that. You know that. But I can't get her to stop. Once she sets her mind on something, she does it."

Every day her father would come home from the fields. He would wash the dust off; he would put on his favorite slippers. They would slap against his heels as he walked to his chair. Then, with a sigh, he would sit down and prop his feet up.

"If you have a comfortable pair of slippers," he liked to say, "you can feel like a king."

She shook her head. "Your royal slippers are falling apart. You need new ones."

Her father stared down at his raggedy slippers. "They're like me,

getting on in years. But we've grown comfortable together."

She picked up her needle. "I'll start now."

"You should be making them for your husband," her father said. "It's time you were married, and I think I have just the man. He's a guest of the Golden Mountain, with his own store over there. I've talked to other people, and he seems like a good person. He's willing to come back to China to marry you."

"But who'll take care of you?" the daughter wondered tearfully.

"I'm an old man with almost all of his life behind him," her father said in exasperation.

"I would give up some of my own life to extend yours," the girl said.

The father shushed her. "You never know what spirits might be listening." He studied her for a moment and then nodded. "If you feel that way, I'll try not to leave you. But you have to get married."

"Yes," the daughter promised.

But her father was very old and died before she could finish the new pair of slippers. The daughter put on the white of mourning and buried her father.

Life became very hard for her after that. Although she worked in the fields all day, she was a tenant farmer, so most of what she grew went to her landlord. As a result, she had very little to eat. Every night, to forget her hunger, she would work on her father's slippers. Because she could not even afford lamp oil or candles, she worked by the light of the moon.

Finally she put the last stitch into the phoenixes embroidered on the slippers. They were the finest she had ever made, but she refused to sell them. Instead, she left them in her father's room with his other things. She was going to throw out his old slippers, but she couldn't part with them either. So she left both pairs of slippers side by side.

That night she woke up to a strange noise. *Slap. Slap. Slap.*

Monsters did not frighten her one bit. She got up from her sleeping mat and lit a candle. She looked all around the house and the kitchen but saw nothing.

She heard the slapping noise other nights, and always at the same time. She always got up and looked all over the house, but she never found anything.

A few months later, the guest left the land of the Golden Mountain and returned to China. She met him under the watchful eye of the matchmaker.

"I know I'm not as exciting as most men," the guest said. "I don't smoke or drink or gamble. But you'll find me steady enough. I like nothing better than to sit down in my favorite chair with a pair of slippers on my feet."

"And do you feel like a prince then?" the woman asked.

"I suppose I could," the guest smiled, "with the right woman. Make me a pair of your famous slippers. That's all I want as your dowry."

The matchmaker looked shocked, but the woman was beginning to like this guest. "I thought you were smarter than that."

"I'm smart enough to know quality. And that's what you are. You were loyal to your father, and you'll be loyal to your husband."

And he began to tell her about his travels and the land of the Golden Mountain.

"I've never been farther than ten kilometers in my life," she said thoughtfully. "It would be exciting to travel and see new lands."

"Then marry me," the guest said.

She shook her head. "People would say I was just marrying you to end my troubles."

"If you marry me, it won't be all that easy," he said. "There aren't many women over there. It can be lonely for a wife overseas. The Americans make it hard for Chinese to bring their wives over."

"Then how come you can do it?" she asked.

"I own a store," the guest explained. "That puts me in a different class."

"When you're the only child of elderly parents," she said, "you get used to being on your own."

The guest just grinned. "I knew you were quality when I saw you."

One meeting led to another. Before she knew it, the woman had come to love the guest. She made a new pair of slippers and gave it to him. They were married shortly afterward. Then she packed up her father's things and stored them away.

It was not as hard as it had once been to reach America, but it was still difficult. It was even harder to get into America. She was questioned closely. But her husband could hire the best American lawyers, so eventually she was freed.

He led her into Chinatown — a strange place. There were American buildings to which the Chinese had added their own decorations —

balconies and shutters and other things. But it was still like seeing a strange face in Chinese costume.

And from there they journeyed on a boat far into the middle of the province to a tiny Chinatown of a few buildings. Beside their store, one was a temple and meeting place. Another was a restaurant. And two were buildings where the Chinese workers slept.

She was the only woman for twenty kilometers. The loneliness and strangeness were terrible things like shadowy monsters that clutched at her. But even so, she refused to give in. She busied herself unpacking her trunk and rearranging the house to suit her taste.

But that night, as she lay on the odd American bed with her husband, she could not sleep. The loneliness closed in on her again. She listened to the alien insects and smelled the strange, new flowers outside her window. And she felt terribly homesick.

But then she heard a familiar sound that made her even more homesick. *Slap. Slap. Slap.*

"What's that?" Her husband lit the American kerosene lantern, and together they searched the whole store, but there was no one there.

"I used to hear it in China too," the woman said.

Her husband scratched his head. "I would have sworn I heard the sound of slippers slapping at someone's heels."

There in the middle of their parlor on the second story was a pair of old slippers.

"He kept his promise. He was coming back all this time, but I didn't understand it." She picked up her father's slippers from the floor and put them in their bedroom. And she didn't feel nearly so alone.

And after that at the same hour every day she would hear the slapping sound of her father's slippers.

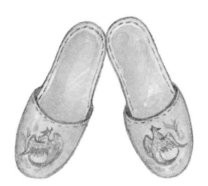

About the Authors

Louisa May Alcott

Louisa May Alcott was born in Germantown, Philadelphia, in 1832 and spent most of her early years in Boston and Concord. Alcott's first book, *Flower Fables* (1855) was written when she was 16 years old and published when she was 23.

Alcott's books for children include: *An Old-Fashioned Girl* (1870), *Little Men* (1871), *Eight Cousins* (1875), *Rose in Bloom* (1876) and *Jo's Boys and How They Turned Out* (1886).

L. Frank Baum

Born in Chittenango, New York, in 1856, Lyman Frank Baum was privately tutored at home and then attended Peekskill Military Academy. Baum is best known for his fantasies for children, particularly *The Wonderful Wizard of Oz* (1900).

The 13 sequels to *The Wonderful Wizard of Oz* include: *The Marvelous Land of Oz* (1904), *Ozma of Oz* (1907), *The Road to Oz* (1909), *The Emerald City of Oz* (1910) and *The Lost Princess of Oz* (1917).

Rosemary Carr Benét

Rosemary (Carr) Benét was born in 1900. In the early 1920s, she was a reporter on the European edition of the *Chicago Tribune*. She met her future husband, poet and novelist Stephen Vincent Benét, in Paris at that time.

Stephen Vincent Benét

Stephen Vincent Benét was born in Bethlehem, Pennsylvania, in 1898. In 1915, when he was 17, his first volume of poetry was published. His first novel, *The Beginning of Wisdom*, was published soon after he graduated from Yale University.

Some of Benét's many volumes of poetry include: *Heavens and Earth* (1920), *King David* (1923), *The Ballad of William Sycamore, 1790-1880* (1923) and *Tiger Joy* (1925). His five novels include: *Jean Huguenot* (1923) and *Spanish Bayonet* (1926).

Arna Bontemps

Born in Alexandria, Louisiana, in 1902, Arna (Arnaud) Bontemps was educated in California. After graduating from Pacific Union College in 1923, he became a teacher and began his writing career. His fiction, anthologies and histories helped to increase interest in African-American literature and culture. He died in 1973.

Bontemps' books for children include: *You Can't Pet a Possum* (1934), *Story of George Washington Carver* (1954) and, with Jack Conroy, *Sam Patch, the High, Wide & Handsome Jumper* (1951).

Betsy Byars

Betsy (Cromer) Byars, a popular writer of novels for children, was born in Charlotte, North Carolina, in 1928. Her first book, *Clementine*, was published in 1962. She has won numerous awards, including the 1971 John Newbery Medal of the American Library Association for *The Summer of the Swans* (1970).

Her children's novels include: *The House of Wings* (1972), *The Golly Sisters Go West* (1986) and *Blossom and the Green Phantom* (1987).

Richard Chase

Born near Huntsville, Alabama, in 1904, Chase was an author, compiler and editor.

Chase collected and retold traditional stories in such books as *The Jack Tales* (1943), *Grandfather Tales: American-English Folk Tales* and *Billy Boy* (1966). He wrote *Jack and the Three Sillies* (1950) and *Wicked John and the Devil* (1951).

Beverly Cleary

Beverly (Bunn) Cleary was born in McMinnville, Oregon, in 1916. Her popular children's books have been published in over ten countries and have won numerous awards, including several Young Readers' Choice Awards and the American Library Association's Laura Ingalls Wilder Award.

Cleary's books include: *Henry Huggins* (1950), *Beezus and Ramona* (1955), *Fifteen* (1956), *Runaway Ralph* (1970) and *Ramona Forever* (1984).

Caroline Cunningham

Caroline Cunningham is the author of *The Talking Stone*, which was published in 1939.

Emily Dickinson

Emily (Elizabeth) Dickinson, born in 1830 in Amherst, Massachusetts, was the daughter of a prominent lawyer. After studying at Amherst Academy and Mount Holyoke Female Seminary, she lived quietly for the rest of her life at her parents' home. Collections of her poetry were published from 1890 to 1896, and she was subsequently recognized as one of the finest lyric poets in the English language.

Collections of Dickinson's poems selected for children include: *Poems for Youth* (edited by Alfred Leete Hampson, 1934), *A Letter to the World: Poems for Young Readers* (edited by R. Godden, 1968) and *I'm Nobody! Who Are You?* (introduced by Richard B. Sewall, 1978).

Walter Farley

Walter Lorimer Farley was born in Syracuse, New York, in 1920. From an early age he had a passion for horses. While attending Columbia University, he wrote his first book, *The Black Stallion*, which was published in 1941.

Farley's books include: *The Black Stallion and Flame* (1960), *The Black Stallion and the Girl* (1971) and *The Black Stallion Legend* (1983).

Robert Frost

Born in San Francisco in 1874, Robert Lee Frost moved to New England with his family at the age of ten. After attending Dartmouth College and Harvard University, he worked at a variety of jobs — making shoes, working in a mill, editing a country newspaper, teaching school and farming. He moved to England in 1912, where he published his first book of poetry. Upon returning to the United States in 1915, he became professor of English at Amherst College.

Frost's poetry collections include: *Twilight* (1894), *North of Boston* (1914), *Mountain Interval* (1916), *West-Running Brook* (1928), *You Come Too: Favorite Poems for Young Readers* (1959) and *In the Clearing* (1962).

Eloise Greenfield

Eloise Greenfield was born in 1929 in Parmele, North Carolina. She published her first poem in 1963 and joined the District of Columbia Black Writers' Workshop, where she later became director of adult fiction (1971-1973) and director of children's literature (1973-1974).

Greenfield's novels and biographies for children include: *Rosa Parks* (1973), *Sister* (1974) and *Paul Robeson* (1975).

Lucretia Peabody Hale

Born in 1820, in Boston, Hale was educated at Elizabeth Peabody's and George

B. Emerson's School. The first story of the "Peterkin Papers" appeared in *Our Young Folks* in 1866, and in 1880 the stories were collected in book form.

Langston Hughes

James Mercer Langston Hughes was born in 1902 in Joplin, Missouri, and attended Lincoln University. During his long and distinguished career, he wrote poetry, lyrics, drama, history, comedy, autobiography and film scripts. His collections of poetry include: *The Weary Blues* (1926), *The Negro Mother and Other Dramatic Recitations* (1931), *A New Song* (1938), *Shakespeare in Harlem* (1942), *Montage of a Dream Deferred* (1951) and *Ask Your Mama: 12 Moods for Jazz* (1961). Hughes died in 1967.

Books of interest to young readers include: *Popo and Fifina: Children of Haiti* (1932), *The First Book of Jazz* (1955; updated in 1976) and *Don't You Turn Back: Poems* (1969).

Washington Irving

Born in New York City in 1783, Irving was the youngest of 11 children. By 1815, he was known as an author, essayist and society gentleman. *The Sketch Book* (1819-1820), which contains "Rip Van Winkle" and "The Legend of Sleepy Hollow," is considered his most important work.

Richard Kennedy

Richard Jerome Kennedy was born in Jefferson City, Missouri, in 1932.

Kennedy's books for children include: *The Blue Stone* (1976), *The Lost Kingdom of Karnica* (1979), *Inside My Feet: The Story of a Giant* (1979) and *Amy's Eyes* (1985).

Henry Wadsworth Longfellow

Born in Portland, Maine, in 1807, Longfellow was educated in private schools and at Bowdoin College. In 1835, he became Smith Professor of Modern Languages at Harvard, where he taught until 1854. His first book of poetry, *Voices of the Night*, was published in 1839. In the years that followed, his poetry became famous abroad as well as in his own country.

Longfellow's collections of poetry include: *Voices of the Night* (1839), *Ballads and Other Poems* (1841), *Evangeline, A Tale of Acadie* (1847), *The Song of Hiawatha* (1855) and *Tales of a Wayside Inn* (1863).

Edna St. Vincent Millay

Born in Rockland, Maine, in 1892, Millay graduated from Vassar College in 1917. She won acclaim for her poetry with the publication of her first collection, *Renascence and Other Poems* (1917). In 1943 the Poetry Society of America awarded her a medal for her contribution to the humanities. She died in 1950.

Among her many books of poetry are: *Second April* (1921), *The Buck in the Snow and Other Poems* (1928), *Wine from These Grapes* (1934) and *Collected Lyrics* (1943).

Ogden Nash

Ogden Frederic Nash was born in Rye, New York, in 1902. Nash became famous for his unconventional rhymes and published numerous volumes of poetry. He died in 1971.

Nash's volumes of poetry for children include: *Parents Keep Out: Elderly Poems for Youngerly Readers* (1951), *The Boy Who Laughed at Santa Claus* (1957) and *The New Nutcracker Suite, and Other Innocent Verses* (1962).

Katherine Paterson

Katherine Womeldorf Paterson was born in 1932 in Qing Jiang, China, where her parents were Presbyterian missionaries. She graduated from King College in Tennessee and obtained a master's degree from the Presbyterian School of Christian Education in Virginia. Paterson has won numerous awards, including the 1977 National Book Award for *The Master Puppeteer* (1976), the Newbery Medal in 1978 for *Bridge to Terabithia* (1977) and the Newbery Medal in 1981 for *Jacob Have I Loved* (1980).

Jack Prelutsky

Born in 1940 in Brooklyn, New York, Prelutsky attended Hunter College in New York. He has published more than 30 poetry collections, which have won many awards.

Prelutsky's books include: *The Terrible Tiger* (1970), *The New Kid on the Block* (1984) and *Twickham Tweer* (1991).

James Whitcomb Riley

Riley was born in Greenfield, Indiana, in 1849. His first poem was published in the Indianapolis *Journal* in 1877, the same year he became assistant editor of the Anderson *Democrat*. Four years later, he published his first book of poetry, *The Old Swimmin' Hole and 'Leven More Poems*. He died in 1916.

Riley's books for children include: *Out to Old Aunt Mary's* (1903), *A Defective Santa Claus* (1904) and *Riley Child Verse* (1908).

Carl Sandburg

Carl August Sandburg was born in Galesburg, Illinois, in 1878. During his career, he published more than 40 books, including a monumental biography of Abraham Lincoln, *Life of Abraham Lincoln* (1926-1939). He died in 1967.

His books for children include: *Rootabaga Stories* (1923), *Abe Lincoln Grows Up* (1928) and *The Wedding Procession of the Rag Doll and the Broom Handle and Who Was in It* (1967).

Shel Silverstein

Shelby Silverstein was born in Chicago in 1932. He is a cartoonist, composer, folk singer and writer. Silverstein has published numerous books of poetry illustrated with his own drawings.

His books include: *The Giving Tree* (1964), *Where the Sidewalk Ends* (1974), *The Missing Piece* (1976) and *A Light in the Attic* (1981).

Mark Twain

Twain was born Samuel Langhorne Clemens in Florida, Missouri, in 1835. His family moved to Hannibal, where he attended school until his father's death in 1847. After traveling for several years, he became a steamboat pilot on the Mississippi. His humorous articles in newspapers and magazines became very popular.

Some of Twain's best-loved books include: *The Adventures of Tom Sawyer* (1876), *The Prince and the Pauper* (1881), *The Adventures of Huckleberry Finn* (1884) and *A Connecticut Yankee in King Arthur's Court* (1889).

Wallace Wadsworth

Born in Indiana in 1894, Wadsworth lived most of his life in Indianapolis. Educated at Butler University, he became a publisher's representative for several publishing houses.

His books include: *Paul Bunyan and His Great Blue Ox* (1926) and *The Modern Story Book* (1931).

Kate Douglas Wiggin

Kate Douglas (Smith) Wiggin was born in Philadelphia in 1856. Although she also wrote adult novels and plays, she is best remembered as the author of *Rebecca of Sunnybrook Farm* (1903) and its sequel, *New Chronicles of Rebecca* (1907). She died in 1923.

Wiggin's novels for children include: *The Birds' Christmas Carol* (1887), *Susanna and Sue* (1909), *Mother Carey's Chickens* (1911) and *The Spirit of Christmas* (1927).

Laura Ingalls Wilder

Laura (Ingalls) Wilder was born near Pepin, Wisconsin, in 1867. When she was a child, her family moved west through Kansas, Minnesota and the Dakotas homesteading. 1932. Her first book, *Little House in the Big Woods*, was published in 1932. *On the Banks of Plum Creek* (1937) and *The Long Winter* (1940) were both Newbery Honor Books. She died in 1957.

Other books Wilder wrote include: *Little House on the Prairie* (1935) and *Little Town on the Prairie* (1941).

Laurence Yep

Born in 1948 in San Francisco, Laurence Michael Yep graduated from the University of California, Santa Cruz. His first book, *Sweetwater*, a science fiction novel, was published in 1973. *Dragonwings* (1975) was a 1976 Newbery Honor Book.

His many books for children include: *Child of the Owl* (1977), *Sea Glass* (1979), *Dragon Steel* (1985) and *Tongues of Jade* (1991).

Jane Yolen

Born in 1939 in New York City, Jane (Hyatt) Yolen had her first stories published in magazines and newspapers while studying at Smith College. Her first book, *Pirates in Petticoats*, was published in 1963.

Yolen's books include: *The Witch Who Wasn't* (1964), *Dream Weaver and Other Tales* (1979), *Sleeping Ugly* (1981) and *Honkers* (1993).

THE ILLUSTRATORS

Jon Davis
"Being Neighborly" (page 70); "Ashes of Roses" (page 100); "Harassing Miss Harris" (page 140); "My People" (page 157); "The Island" (page 194); "Lonesome Boy" (page 236).

Richard Hook
"Nancy Hanks 1784–1818" (page 33); "Jack and the North West Wind" (page 58); "The Wind Begun to Rock the Grass" (page 117); "Little Orphant Annie" (page 138); "Cunning Brer Rabbit" (page 168); "The Scarecrow and the Tin Woodman" (page 218).

John Lupton
"The Little Scarred One" (page 12); "Cap Garland" (page 42); "Hiawatha's Childhood" (page 96); "Coyote and Water Serpent" (page 160); "The Runaway" (page 178); "The Tale of Custard the Dragon" (page 214); "The Pot Child" (page 228).

Valerie Sangster
"Rip Van Winkle" (page 18); "Pirates" (page 86); "Afternoon on a Hill" (page 148); "A Puppy for Harvey" (page 150); "Slippers" (page 250).

Brian Price Thomas
"Pecos Bill" (page 34); "The Contests at Cowlick" (page 120); "The Peterkins Are Obliged to Move" (page 128); "The Wonderful Ox" (page 172); "Henry and Ribs" (page 180); "The Huckabuck Family . . ." (page 208); "An Irritating Creature" (page 226).

The work of the above artists is by courtesy of Linden Artists, London.

Shel Silverstein
"Zebra Question" (page 205).

ACKNOWLEDGMENTS

Care has been taken to trace ownership of copyright material contained in this book. The publishers will gladly receive any information that will enable them to rectify any reference or credit line in subsequent editions.

"Afternoon on a Hill" by Edna St. Vincent Millay (page 148). From *Edna St. Vincent Millay's Poems Selected For Young People* by Edna St. Vincent Millay. Copyright © 1917, 1921, 1922, 1923, 1929, 1949, 1950, 1951 by Edna St. Vincent Millay. Copyright © 1951 by Ronald Keller. Reprinted by permission of Fitzhenry & Whiteside Limited.

"Ashes of Roses" by Kate Douglas Wiggin (page 100). From *Rebecca of Sunnybrook Farm* by Kate Douglas Wiggin. From *Rebecca of Sunnybrook Farm* published by Dell Publishing, afterword copyright © 1986 by Paula Danziger.

"Being Neighborly" by Louisa May Alcott (page 70). Excerpt from *Little Women* by Louisa May Alcott (Puffin Books, 1953).

"Cap Garland" by Laura Ingalls Wilder (page 42). Excerpt from *The Long Winter* by Laura Ingalls Wilder. Copyright © 1940 by Laura Ingalls Wilder, renewed © 1968 by Roger L. MacBride. Reprinted by permission of HarperCollins Publishers.

"The Contests at Cowlick" by Richard Kennedy (page 120). Excerpt from *Richard Kennedy: Collected Stories* by Richard Kennedy. Copyright © 1987 by Richard Kennedy. Reprinted by permission of HarperCollins Publishers.

"Harassing Miss Harris" by Katherine Paterson (page 140). Excerpt from *The Great Gilly Hopkins* by Katherine Paterson. Copyright © 1978 by Katherine Paterson. Reprinted by permission of HarperCollins Publishers.

"Henry and Ribs" by Beverly Cleary (page 180). From *Henry Huggins* by Beverly Cleary. Copyright © 1950 by William Morrow & Company, Inc. Renewed © 1978 by Beverly Cleary. By permission of Morrow Junior Books, a division of William Morrow & Company, Inc.

"Hiawatha's Childhood" by H.W. Longfellow (page 96). Excerpt from *The Song of Hiawatha* by H.W. Longfellow (J.M. Dent & Sons Ltd., 1960).

"The Huckabuck Family and How They Raised Popcorn in Nebraska and Quit and Came Back" by Carl Sandburg (page 208). From *Rootabaga Stories* by Carl Sandburg, copyright © 1923, 1922 by Harcourt Brace Jovanovich, Inc. and renewed 1951, 1950 by Carl Sandburg, reprinted by permission of the publisher.

"An Irritating Creature" by Jack Prelutsky (page 226). From *The New Kid on the Block* by Jack Prelutsky. Copyright © 1984 by Jack Prelutsky. By permission of Greenwillow Books, a division of William Morrow & Company, Inc.

"The Island" by Walter Farley (page 194). From *The Black Stallion* by Walter Farley. Copyright © 1941 and renewed 1969 by Walter Farley. Reprinted by permission of Random House, Inc.

"Jack and the North West Wind" by Richard Chase (page 58). From *The Jack Tales* by Richard Chase. Copyright © 1943, renewed 1971 by Richard Chase. Reprinted by permission of Houghton Mifflin Company. All rights reserved.

"Little Orphant Annie" by James Whitcomb Riley (page 138). From *Joyful Poems for Children* by James Whitcomb Riley, copyright © 1941, 1946 and 1960 by Lesley Payne, Elizabeth Eitel Miesse and Edmund H. Eitel. Published by Bobbs-Merrill Company, Inc.

"The Little Scarred One" by Caroline Cunningham (page 12). From *The Talking Stone* by Caroline Cunningham. Copyright © 1939 by Alfred A. Knopf, Inc. Copyright © renewed 1967 by Caroline Cunningham. Reprinted by permission of Alfred A. Knopf, Inc.

"Lonesome Boy" by Arna Bontemps (page 236). From *Lonesome Boy* by Arna Bontemps. Copyright © 1955 by Arna Bontemps and Feliks Topolski. Copyright © renewed 1983 by Arna Bontemps. Copyright © renewed 1987 by Feliks Topolski. Reprinted by permission of Houghton Mifflin Company. All rights reserved.

"My People" by Langston Hughes (page 157). From *The Dreamkeeper* by Langston Hughes. Copyright © 1932 by Alfred A. Knopf, Inc. Reprinted by permission of Alfred A. Knopf, Inc.

"Nancy Hanks 1784–1818" by Rosemary Carr and Stephen Vincent Benét (page 33). From *A Book of Americans*, published by Rinehart & Company, Inc. Copyright © 1933, by Rosemary Carr and Stephen Vincent Benét.

"Pecos Bill" is a traditional tall tale from the American southwest, retold by S.E. Renouf (page 34). Copyright © 1994 S.E. Renouf. Reprinted by permission of S.E. Renouf.

"The Peterkins Are Obliged to Move" by Lucretia P. Hale (page 128). From *The Peterkin Papers* by Lucretia P. Hale. First published 1880.

"Pirates" by Mark Twain (page 86). Excerpt from *The Adventures of Tom Sawyer* (Puffin Books, 1950).

"The Pot Child" by Jane Yolen (page 228). Reprinted by permission of Philomel Books from *Dream Weaver* by Jane Yolen. "The Pot Child" copyright © 1978 by Jane Yolen.

"A Puppy for Harvey" by Betsy Byars (page 150). Excerpt from *The Pinballs* by Betsy Byars. Copyright © 1977 by Betsy Byars. Reprinted by permission of HarperCollins Publishers.

"Rip Van Winkle" by Washington Irving (page 18). Excerpt from *Rip Van Winkle and Other Stories* by Washington Irving (Puffin Books, 1986).

"The Runaway" by Robert Frost (page 178). From *You Come Too* by Robert Frost. Copyright © 1959 Holt, Rinehart and Winston, Inc. Copyright © renewed 1964 by Lesley Frost Ballantine.

"The Scarecrow and The Tin Woodman" by L. Frank Baum (page 218). From *Little Wizard Stories of Oz* by L. Frank Baum. Copyright © 1913 by L. Frank Baum and 1914 by the Reilly & Britton Co.; copyright © renewed 1941 by Maude Gage Baum. This version copyright © 1985 by the Baum Trust.

"Slippers" by Laurence Yep (page 250). Excerpt from *The Rainbow People* by Laurence Yep. Copyright © 1989 by Laurence Yep. Reprinted by permission of HarperCollins Publishers.

"The Tale of Custard the Dragon" by Ogden Nash (page 214). From *Verses From 1929 On* by Ogden Nash. Copyright © 1936 by Ogden Nash. By permission of Little, Brown and Company.

"Way Down In The Music" by Eloise Greenfield (page 147). Excerpt from *Honey, I Love* by Eloise Greenfield. Copyright © 1978 by Eloise Greenfield. Reprinted by permission of HarperCollins Publishers.

"The Wind Begun to Rock the Grass" by Emily Dickinson (page 117). Reprinted by permission of the publishers and the Trustees of Amherst College from *The Poems of Emily Dickinson*, Thomas H. Johnson, ed. (Cambridge, Mass.: The Belknap Press of Harvard University Press), copyright © 1951, 1955, 1979, 1983 by the President and Fellows of Harvard College.

"The Wonderful Ox" by Wallace Wadsworth (page 172). Excerpt from *Paul Bunyan and the Great Blue Ox* by Wallace Wadsworth, copyright © 1926 by Doubleday, a division of Bantam Doubleday Dell Publishing Group, Inc. Used by permission of the publisher.

"Zebra Question" text and art by Shel Silverstein (page 205). Excerpt from *A Light in the Attic* by Shel Silverstein. Copyright © 1981 by Evil Eye Music, Inc. Reprinted by permission of HarperCollins Publishers.

INDEX

Adventure
  "Cap Garland" (Laura Ingalls
    Wilder), 42
  "The Island" (Walter Farley), 194
  "Pirates" (Mark Twain), 86
"Afternoon on a Hill" (Edna St.
  Vincent Millay), 148
Alcott, Louisa May, 258: "Being
  Neighborly," 70
Animal Stories
  "Coyote and Water Serpent"
    (Traditional), 160
  "Cunning Brer Rabbit"
    (Traditional), 168
  "Henry and Ribs" (Beverly
    Cleary), 180
  "The Island" (Walter Farley), 194
  "The Wonderful Ox" (Wallace
    Wadsworth), 172
"Ashes of Roses" (Kate Douglas
  Wiggin), 100

Baum, L. Frank, 258: "The Scarecrow
  and the Tin Woodman," 218
"Being Neighborly" (Louisa May
  Alcott), 70
Benét, Rosemary Carr, 258: "Nancy
  Hanks 1784–1818," 33

Benét, Stephen Vincent, 258: "Nancy
  Hanks 1784–1818," 33
Bontemps, Arna, 259: "Lonesome
  Boy," 236
Byars, Betsy, 259: "A Puppy for
  Harvey," 150

"Cap Garland" (Laura Ingalls Wilder),
  42
Chase, Richard, 259: "Jack and the
  North West Wind," 58
Cleary, Beverly, 259: "Henry and
  Ribs," 180
"The Contests at Cowlick" (Richard
  Kennedy), 120
"Coyote and Water Serpent"
  (Traditional), 160
"Cunning Brer Rabbit" (Traditional),
  168
Cunningham, Caroline, 259: "The
  Little Scarred One," 12

Dickinson, Emily, 260: "The Wind
  Begun to Rock the Grass," 117

Fantasy
  "Lonesome Boy" (Arna Bontemps),
    236

"Rip Van Winkle" (Washington Irving), 18

"The Scarecrow and the Tin Woodman" (L. Frank Baum), 218

"Slippers" (Laurence Yep), 250

Farley, Walter, 260: "The Island," 194

Folktales
"Cunning Brer Rabbit" (Traditional), 168
"Jack and the North West Wind" (Richard Chase), 58
"Pecos Bill" (Traditional), 34
"The Pot Child" (Jane Yolen), 228
"The Wonderful Ox" (Wallace Wadsworth), 172

Frost, Robert, 260: "The Runaway," 178

Greenfield, Eloise, 260: "Way Down in the Music," 147

Growing Up
"Ashes of Roses" (Kate Douglas Wiggin), 100
"Being Neighborly" (Louisa May Alcott), 70
"Harassing Miss Harris" (Katherine Paterson), 140
"A Puppy for Harvey" (Betsy Byars), 150

Hale, Lucretia P., 260: "The Peterkins Are Obliged to Move," 128

"Harassing Miss Harris" (Katherine Paterson), 140

"Henry and Ribs" (Beverly Cleary), 180

"Hiawatha's Childhood" (H.W. Longfellow), 96

"The Huckabuck Family . . ." (Carl Sandburg), 208

Hughes, Langston, 261: "My People," 157

Humor
"The Contests at Cowlick" (Richard Kennedy), 120
"Henry and Ribs" (Beverly Cleary), 180
"The Huckabuck Family . . ." (Carl Sandburg), 208
"Jack and the North West Wind" (Richard Chase), 58
"Pecos Bill" (Traditional), 34
"The Peterkins Are Obliged to Move" (Lucretia P. Hale), 128

"An Irritating Creature" (Jack Prelutsky), 226

Irving, Washington, 261: "Rip Van Winkle," 18

"The Island" (Walter Farley), 194

"Jack and the North West Wind" (Richard Chase), 58

Kennedy, Richard, 261: "The Contests at Cowlick," 120

Legends
"Coyote and Water Serpent" (Traditional), 160
"The Little Scarred One" (Caroline Cunningham), 12
"Little Orphant Annie" (James Whitcomb Riley), 138
"The Little Scarred One" (Caroline Cunningham), 12
"Lonesome Boy" (Arna Bontemps), 236

Longfellow, H.W., 261: "Hiawatha's Childhood," 96

Millay, Edna St. Vincent, 261:
    "Afternoon on a Hill," 148
"My People" (Langston Hughes), 157

"Nancy Hanks 1784–1818"
    (Rosemary Carr and Stephen
    Vincent Benét), 33
Nash, Ogden, 262: "The Tale of
    Custard the Dragon," 214

Paterson, Katherine, 262: "Harassing
    Miss Harris," 140
"Pecos Bill" (Traditional), 34
"The Peterkins Are Obliged to Move"
    (Lucretia P. Hale), 128
"Pirates" (Mark Twain), 86
Poetry
    "Afternoon on a Hill" (Edna St.
        Vincent Millay), 148
    "Hiawatha's Childhood"
        (H.W. Longfellow), 96
    "An Irritating Creature"
        (Jack Prelutsky), 226
    "Nancy Hanks 1784–1818"
        (Rosemary Carr and Stephen
        Vincent Benét), 33
    "Little Orphant Annie" (James
        Whitcomb Riley), 138
    "My People" (Langston Hughes),
        157
    "The Runaway" (Robert Frost),
        178
    "The Tale of Custard the Dragon"
        (Ogden Nash), 214
    "Way Down in the Music" (Eloise
        Greenfield), 147
    "The Wind Begun to Rock the
        Grass" (Emily Dickinson), 117
    "Zebra Question" (Shel Silverstein),
        205

"The Pot Child" (Jane Yolen), 228
Prelutsky, Jack, 262: "An Irritating
    Creature," 226
"A Puppy for Harvey" (Betsy Byars),
    150

Riley, James Whitcomb, 262: "Little
    Orphant Annie," 138
"Rip Van Winkle" (Washington
    Irving), 18
"The Runaway" (Robert Frost), 178

Sandburg, Carl, 262: "The Huckabuck
    Family . . .," 208
"The Scarecrow and the Tin
    Woodman" (L. Frank Baum), 218
Silverstein, Shel, 263: "Zebra
    Question," 205
"Slippers" (Laurence Yep), 250

"The Tale of Custard the Dragon"
    (Ogden Nash), 214
Twain, Mark, 263: "Pirates," 86

Wadsworth, Wallace, 263: "The
    Wonderful Ox," 172
"Way Down in the Music" (Eloise
    Greenfield), 147
Wiggin, Kate Douglas, 263: "Ashes of
    Roses," 100
Wilder, Laura Ingalls, 263: "Cap
    Garland," 42
"The Wind Begun to Rock the Grass"
    (Emily Dickinson), 117
"The Wonderful Ox" (Wallace
    Wadsworth), 172

Yep, Laurence, 264: "Slippers," 250
Yolen, Jane, 264: "The Pot Child,"
    228